LET THE DAY PERISH

LET THE DAY PERISH

stories by
CHRISTIAN PETERSEN

Porcepic Books
an imprint of

Beach Holme Publishing
Vancouver

This book is published by Beach Holme Publishing, #226—2040 West 12th Ave., Vancouver, BC, V6J 2G2. This is a Porcepic Book.

We acknowledge the financial support of the Canada Council for the Arts, the Government of Canada through the Book Publishing Industry Development Program (BPIDP) and the assistance of the Province of British Columbia through the British Columbia Arts Council for our publishing activities and program.

The Canada Council | Le Conseil des Arts
for the Arts | du Canada
since 1957 | depuis 1957

Canada

Editor: Joy Gugeler
Cover Design: Teresa Bubela
Type Design: Jen Hamilton
Author Photograph: Ann Smith
Cover Art: Sculpture by Casey McGlynn. 42" x 38", steel, wood. Used with permission of the artist.

Canadian Cataloguing in Publication Data

Petersen, Christian.
  Let the day perish

ISBN 0-88878-400-7

  I. Title.
PS8581.E83L47 1999   C813'.54   C99-910886-7
PR9199.3.P452L47 1999

For Jean, and for Kidda,
in memory.

For Ann,
in every breath.

CONTENTS

I'm going out where the lights don't shine so bright,
when I get back you can treat me like a Saturday night.
  —"Treat Me Like A Saturday Night", Jimmie Dale Gilmore

If a story is not to be about love or fear, then I think it must
be about anger.
  —"The Look of the Lightning, The Sound of the Birds",
                                          Diane Schoemperlen

HEART RED MONACO

He yanks the night back like a ragtop. The splintered windshield is tinged with chlorine light, dawn of the third Sunday in July. They speed over the steel beam bridge, above the green current, through the river mist and mill steam. As the car growls up the hill south of town stars are just fading in the rearview mirror, way back in the purple-black west of Nazko country.

Thomas whispers, "I'll sleep when I'm dead." He grins, half a cigarette gently clenched between ivory teeth. Then he squints his dark eyes and casually with his left hand rips the old car screeching off the highway, down through the scarred log arch entrance to the rodeo grounds. The Monaco crow-hops in the dirt ruts, raising a flurry of dust. Muscled quarter horses stand tethered to aluminum trailers, curtains are drawn in the cowboys' campers, and the pickup trucks wear wry chrome smiles. He cuts the headlights. They approach the warped backside of the wooden arena and the corrals where the circuit bucking stock is held, the longhorn bulls and the broncs. There is an over-rich focus to it all, a lingering chemical static in the blood, sporadic shooting flares of hyper green joy, then icy fear, joy, fear.

In his jean jacket Ben slouches against the passenger door, shivers slightly, rubs his knuckles in his eyes as the silent tires press over the turf. In draughts through the car vents come scents of trampled bluegrass, fresh-cut sawdust and horseshit. His mind feels rinsed and his body aroused by the night spent on psilocybin. Thomas exhales the spicy smoke of his Winstons.

Six feet from the corral fence the wide red car halts and the V8 idles quietly for a few seconds. Thomas' hand brushes the dash and turns off the key. Silence rushes the windows. Thomas searches the floor and finds the J&B, very last of it. Ben declines. Thomas downs it, then drops the empty green bottle over his shoulder, thuds behind the seat. Anger suddenly fills the car interior. Ben has to get out, open the door, swing his boots in the grass. He stands and leans against the unfailing body of the car, slides forward, hauls up and sits on the hood with his back against the windshield. The cooling engine ticks twice. The drugs are wearing off smoothly and the sky is now precious silver. After a time Thomas joins him, their legs stretch out down the hood of the Monaco and the big light at the end of the rodeo arena makes their boots shine. Lizard and leather.

The animals are quiet inside the corral, a faint steam rises from their broad warm backs, the bulls have settled in deep sawdust nests and the broncs doze neck to neck. The horses are roughened and musky. Just one is wide awake, curious and stepping forward. He's a dark buckskin, with a black mane and tail, black legs, and his thick neck arched attentively. Thomas lights another Winston, the quick flame startles the horse. He swings his head, his muscles roll and the line of his strong flank deepens as he wheels away.

◆ ◆ ◆

Ben's father was a bush pilot. On the afternoon of October 12, 1979, he got caught in a freak snowstorm and crashed his floatplane while trying to set down on the Blackwater River. The accident made headlines, mostly because his two passengers happened to be the manager of one of the town's largest mills and the representative of a Japanese company looking to invest big money. All three were killed. Some suggested that Ben's father was at fault for flying in bad weather.

At school that following winter Ben stuck to himself, spent lunch hours in the library, and lost touch with his friends. His studies became an escape, from the attention he got after the accident, and from questions he didn't want to answer.

Quesnel was a small place. Rumours ran like stray dogs there, rarely worth much, but sometimes troublesome or mean. And for the rest of the time he spent in that town, the spring of his final year at school and the summer after graduation, it seemed that he lived with different rumours. First about his father, then his mother and Harold Nelson, and finally Ben's own friendship with Thomas Ross.

Those memories seem only one hard all-night drive gone by, though it has been more than fifteen years, and he can't say anything about where Thomas might be now.

♦ ♦ ♦

Another rumour was going around that spring: a volcano had erupted way off in the endless jackpine, about forty miles out the Nazko road, someone said, past Puntschesacut. Apparently from there you could see the smoke, the cone rock lip, rising white ash, orange lava.

"Listen," Ben said, while chalking his pool cue, "you and me could be the first to actually see this thing. This is our big chance." He placed his fingers on the green felt, slid the cue excitedly against the rail, and missed a straight shot at his last highball. Thomas snapped the black eight in the side pocket, and dropped his cue on the table. "Yeah right," he smirked. "Nothin' else to do, I guess."

They climbed into the Monaco, Thomas swung by the Billy Barker Hotel and Ben galloped into the bar to buy a case of beer. They were just eighteen, and still felt as if getting away with that were something.

Thomas was not as keen as Ben about looking for that volcano. Whatever this country offered he took for granted, even mention of white bears, wild mustangs, or spirits that inhabited the canyons and springs of the Itcha mountains. He knew of stranger secrets. His mother was Carrier and as a kid he had lived for a time out on a reserve. He knew that road.

Top down, they blasted out of town, music mixing with the wind. After a fast hour Thomas pulled over onto the gravel shoulder, shut off the engine, stuck out his hand for another beer. He took off his mirrored glasses and glanced up the steepness of the mountain. Then he gave Ben a look which said, "This is going to be a real hike, and it better be worth it."

It was slow going because they were half-drunk and the smooth leather soles of their western boots slipped backwards on the fine speared grass that grew beneath the pines. The ground was very dry, yet the slope was shining with wild grass, blue juniper, and waxy, thorny Oregon grape. Thomas was a ways behind, crisscrossing up the slope with a beer in one hand, sidestepping the rocks so he didn't scuff his boots.

Up ahead, wisps of white smoke rose from a blackened crust of rock into the sharp blue sky.

"I see it!" Ben yelled back excitedly. Thomas' expression didn't change.

There were no splashes of lava, but there was a queer smell. Ben's steps slowed as he got closer, Thomas caught up and stood beside as they peered over the lip.

"You're right, this was some big chance —to see a cave full of smoking bat shit." They laughed and Thomas hurled his beer bottle into the cave. A second passed before it shattered.

Then Thomas turned his gaze and grew silent. Vast pine country swept out before them, countless jagged valleys, and in the distance blue peaks that stretched away like lifelong promise.

♦ ♦ ♦

Thomas had a hard leaning to violence. He was contained like a cougar, and usually he was that quiet. You could never be certain what would set him off. No one in town had the nerve to fight him. Whenever someone got close to it, Thomas would stare at him and softly say, "D'you wanna bad time?" Once a teacher tried to guide him forcibly out of a grade ten gym class. Thomas dropped him to the floor. The man's collarbone broke and Thomas was expelled.

Ben knew him by reputation, but they did not meet until Ben's senior year. Thomas lived in a house-trailer, in a court not far from the senior high school and he sold dope. The trailer was owned by his uncle or someone who was never there. One lunch hour Jimmy Gillis took Ben along to buy a quarter ounce of grass. Thomas was unfriendly and stared at Ben when they entered the trailer. Inside was a worn pool table, hotel surplus with a ratty felt and the wood finish gone, a threadbare couch, and a small black and white TV. After they smoked a joint, Thomas and Ben got talking, turned out they were both Bruins fans.

A few minutes passed and then he looked right at Ben and said, "Your old man, he was in that plane crash?"

"That's right." A chill crept up Ben's neck and he straightened in the chair. Jimmy seemed a bit scared suddenly. "He was the pilot," Ben replied.

Quietly Thomas said, "Nobody coulda known that storm was comin'."

Ben watched his own hands on the table, traced the grain in the arborite with his little finger. Jimmy Gillis was nervous with the silence, and he kept checking his watch, then looking around.

Thomas started to roll another joint, and as he licked the paper his dark eyes held Ben's for just a moment. He said, "Jimmy, you're gonna be late for school." Jimmy Gillis picked up his baggie of dope, looked at Ben curiously, and left.

Thomas lit the second smoke and passed it to Ben. Then he put Lynard Skynard on his stereo and took a bottle of Southern Comfort out of the cupboard. As he poured the liquor into coffee cups he said, "Least you know who your old man was, that's more than I do."

That was in March: sunshine and wind, silver ice still thick on the windows of the trailer. The Bruins lasted as far as the quarter-finals that year.

◆ ◆ ◆

It was around this same time that Harold Nelson began visiting Ben's mother. He sold real estate and sat as alderman on the town council, bought a new car every two years, and considered himself a big wheel. Harold seemed to think the boy needed guidance, and Ben's mother did not discourage him.

The last few months of high school Ben lost interest in his studies and began spending more time with Thomas. Often he left school at lunch hour and spent the afternoon at the trailer. The guys that came to buy dope were puzzled. Ben had been a real school boy, but there he was standing in the kitchen with a bottle of beer, while Thomas divvied up the skunk weed on the table and took their money. They were afraid of Thomas.

One afternoon, when Ben was not there, two patrol cars pulled up to the trailer. When Thomas resisted their search one of them pounded him in the gut with the butt of a shotgun. They didn't find the marijuana, which was stashed in a Cheerios box sitting right on the counter.

♦ ♦ ♦

Thomas and Ben talked of girls, whether the Monaco could make it to Cape Horn, where they might find Dodge parts in South America, the way to properly pass a football. Thomas could be stubborn. He insisted on teaching Ben the things high school did not provide. And he could be funny too. He sometimes asked questions which made Ben laugh, because they were impossible to answer. As if Ben knew one way or the other if there was a God, or what time really meant.

♦ ♦ ♦

The old Texaco garage up from the BCR tracks had been converted into the town's first nightclub, and they often ended up there on a Saturday after midnight, because they had nowhere else to go. Music hammered against the glossy painted walls, and coloured lights flickered at the edge of the dancefloor. They kicked off with tequila, to try and get in the mood, and then drank a mean succession of beers. They grabbed a corner table, out of the way, but Thomas always drew a strange amount of attention. People were wary of him, his cutting eyes like wet chips of shale, his sullenness. Yet they were drawn to him too. Guys wanted to talk about hockey, or bush work or buying dope, anything. Girls asked him to dance, which was not customary. None of this impressed Thomas.

Sitting there, across from him, Ben sometimes felt invisible.

As the snow melted and mild breezes carried into the nights, parties sprung up on the outskirts of town, often at the stockcar track or in a field or a gravel pit. Someone set stereo speakers out on the roof of a pickup and cranked the volume full blast. Hundreds of people crowded around roaring bonfires. Drunken faces hovered in the light. Bottles hurled into the flames hissed and exploded. Rumbling vehicles came and went, with just their parking lights peering through the dust. Now and then somebody passed out in the grass and got run over. Once a young girl was crippled this way.

♦ ♦ ♦

One green evening in June they sat on the steps outside the trailer, looking across the new town development to the bank of the Fraser and its muddy high-water. They'd been stoned and drinking half the day and now faced another aggravated night in town. It was bronze light in the whorls of the river current that made Thomas think of the hotsprings. They yanked the top down and cruised by The Billy for a case of beer.

With a tailwind, that old Dodge could do a hundred and ten miles an hour. But the hotsprings were a fair distance southwest of town, and the rough road slowed them down. By the time they arrived, though the air remained warm, it was dark. In the light of a campfire they saw a new four-wheel-drive parked in the trees, and two couples by the fire.

Weaving around, Thomas and Ben managed to tug off their boots, strip and tiptoe, grinning, into the steamy pool. The water filtered up between the bed stones, and rippled against the pads of their feet. As the current reached the surface it became visible, faintly traced with silver light. On Ben's tongue was the taste of warm coins and beer.

Wanting a cigarette, Thomas turned his shoulders, looking for his shirt which lay just out of reach. He leaned out of the water and stretched his arm toward his Winstons. Thomas' body was chiseled and corded with muscle. He settled back into the water holding the lit cigarette in one raised hand. Ben was staring up at the stars, aware of Thomas watching him. Their hair was curly damp and their faces had begun to sweat.

Before long they were too hot and both pulled themselves out onto the smooth stony bank to cool, leaving just their lower legs submerged.

A woman appeared silently between them at the edge of the spring. Ben shifted forward about to duck into the water when Thomas stopped him with a jab of his dark eyes, taunting.

She waited half a moment, then shucked her hiker's shorts, pulled her t-shirt over her head, and humming softly she lowered her body into the pool. Her breasts swayed and shadows caressed the curve of her belly and thighs. Ben was breathing through his mouth, and could feel the pulse at the back of his knees against the smooth wet rock. She had long coppery hair which she held up with one hand. Then she snugged her neck against the stone rim of the pool. Her white arms circled gently through the water.

They folded under, lifting her breasts while the water lapped between and into the hollow of her throat. When she moved beneath the water, her leg pressed to Ben's.

A breeze parted the steam rising from the spring, and with it drifted the spicy pitch smoke of the fire. Light scampered in the pines like spirits bent on mischief. Thomas was leaning toward the woman with his weight on one rigid arm, and a perfectly calm smile on his face. The woman arched her back, so that for a moment Ben's eyes touched her breasts, then fastened on the stem of her throat. She was smiling too.

"Barbara? Barbara?!" A man's loud voice, angry and very drunk, intruded. Thomas turned his head, a hard glint in his eye.

The woman in the water had an uncertain look on her face. Moments passed. Finally she stood. Her skin had flushed with heat, and the water on her body ran with starlight. Barbara had the good sense to put her clothes back on and return to her husband, though leaving her smile.

◆ ◆ ◆

Dawn of that third Sunday in July —Thomas lights another Winston, the quick flame startles the horse. He swings his head, his muscles roll and the line of his strong flank deepens as he wheels away.

Ben shifts his back, still reclined against the windshield. Thomas turns his head, toward Ben but not far enough to meet his eyes.

Thomas' profile is backlit by the big light at the end of the rodeo arena. Finally he asks, "D'you ever wonder what's gonna happen, you know, later?" Then he looks right at Ben, with fear. His eyes do not waver, while he waits for an answer. All at once the two seem like brothers —fatherless, almost innocent. Ben nods in reply.

Thomas shifts his gaze to the rodeo stock. That buckskin bronc is frisking around with the first rays of light, twisting its meaty neck, and glaring at them. Most of the horses are still dozing. Thomas says, "Fuck it anyway."

Then after a moment his face flashes with a grin. He says, "Hey man, I got an idea." He hops off the hood of the car, swings over the rails of the fence, his shiny lizard boots in the soft sand and sawdust. Like a fool he goes over and opens the gate. He starts walking toward that crazy buckskin and waves his arms. The horse bolts and kicks. He walks around behind clapping his hands. "Gdyap!" He chuckles.

He moves with a sort of strut, but grace as well. The horses throw their heels, they whinny and snort, and their hooves pound as they gallop over the packed dirt of the parking area.

"Heeyeeeeeah! Heee! HEEYEEOOOAHEE!!" Thomas shrieks and howls. Ben stumbles and reels with laughter.

Cowboys and their women step out from the doorways of the campers. Some in their underwear, with legs much whiter than arms, and hair all askew.

Thomas and Ben hightail it for the car.

THE NEXT NINE HUNDRED YEARS

Warren drives forklift. Afternoons this week, and he's just come out the ass end of a bad shift. The mill yard is treacherous in winter, rutted and patched with ice. First he got stuck. That put him behind. Then going too fast he lost a load of 2x10s, and spent twenty minutes swearing, sweating, and stacking those planks back on the forks by hand. He's worked here twelve years, been driving for five, this is only the second load he's ever dumped. That don't stop the foreman's voice squawking over the radio.

Now he's got his lunchkit under his arm and is headed for his pickup.

In the yellow lit parking lot he hears the echo of his name. It's Rick. With a bottle. Ordinarily Warren would wave it off, or maybe have one belt standing beside Rick's Camaro. But tonight, tonight Warren will take him up on it. Sitting in the dark car they kill a mickey of rye, chase it with Coke.

Mothy wet flakes fly in the headlights, streak the windshield on his way home.

Home is a trailer, with an addition which Warren built on. The glow of the porch lamp beckons him from the highway. He stomps his boots in the snow on the path, tries to knock off some of the mud frozen to the sole's black grip. They feel leaden. His balance is slack from the rye.

He steps inside quiet as he can, so as not to wake his wife or the girls. The dog gives a low growl.

"Hush up Joy," he whispers.

Recognizing his voice the shelty runs over, lifts its front paws against Warren's leg. He flicks on the light, sits down heavily on the bench. The porch is cluttered with boots and coats and puppy toys. Laundry is heaped on the washer. For a moment he leans back, rests his head against the wall.

The shelty paws at his legs. Warren scratches her neck. Then pushes her away as he bends over to untie his boots. The laces are frozen. The dog tries to help. "Go on," he shoves her away.

He's got his leg up, tugging off his right boot. The dog jabs her nose in his crotch. Warren swings his left foot, spins her into the corner. Throws his boot. The heel nails the shelty on her ear. She slumps, and shivers on the floor.

"Hey... Joy?" he whispers. "Damn it."

The dog is dead.

Warren lifts her up, carries her out and lays her gently in the box of his pickup. Snowflakes light on her tawny hair. He stands there with his hands on the tailgate for a moment, in his left boot, his sock foot held up as though injured.

Then he hobbles back inside to bed.

At breakfast Cheryl says to him, "Joy's not here hon, she's missing."

Warren is barely awake, but thinks hard, and feigns some puzzlement. "You sure? She must've slipped out last night when I came in. She'll probably show up."

It has snowed five inches overnight, so that the dog is covered over in the back of the pickup. Days go by. It snows more. Warren keeps meaning to go by the dump, or throw her out in the ditch. But after a while it just slips his mind.

Weeks go by, then a chinook brings a sudden melt. That day at coffee-break Dave says, "Warren, that is one dead dog you got in the back of your truck."

The story comes out. That evening, when the road is empty, Warren stops and flings what's left of Joy into the brush. A ratty, shrivelled rind of a dog.

◆ ◆ ◆

Gene rotates. The reason he never works one station for long is simple, and the foremen know it well: nobody likes Gene.

Unfortunately he's got fourteen years IWA seniority. The production crews, the foremen and supervisors, even the office staff keep waiting and hoping, but so far no one has found a valid excuse to fire the guy.

Gene bathes about once a month, lives in a cabin out on a dirtpatch ranch and his well went dry so he has to haul water from town. He's a skinflint, always tries to get things free or wrangle an extra dollar. Last year he raised weiner pigs, selling them to guys at the mill, until it got around that he'd fed them fast food trash, bits of Big Macs, cherry pies, wrappers and cigarette butts. His nostrils are enormous. He wears bottle-thick glasses that shrink his eyes, so he actually looks a lot like his pigs. Constantly chews sunflower seeds, spews them all over, often there is a shell stuck to his chin with saliva. A person gets the feeling that Gene is always horny, in strange ways, from his nervousness, and part of his smell. He talks and talks about himself: his "ranch", the sex he never gets, his unlimited schemes to make an extra dollar.

Gene sells eggs. I wouldn't buy his eggs, but some guys do. He tells them to return the cartons, of course. But eventually the carton supply dwindles. Gene starts whining about this. One day Jasbindur, a planerman, tells Gene he's got a whole stack of egg cartons at home.

"Great," says Gene. "Give them to me."

"You pay ten cents each," says Jas, with a wink in my direction.

"No way," says Gene. Still, for weeks, he keeps pestering Jas about these cartons.

"You pay ten cents."

"No fuckin' way." But finally Gene really needs those cartons, and he tells Jas he'll pay five cents each.

"Sorry," says Jas, smiling, "All recycled." Gene was pissed off, I tell you.

Gene likes to read those newspapers concerning three-headed children and so on. He keeps us all up to date. One shift Gene is reading his paper out loud at coffee. He's all excited that scientists have discovered the antidote to aging. They say people will live and work for a thousand years or more. Down the table sits Mike, who has worked here thirty-odd years and has one more to go before his retirement. Old Mike rarely speaks. But this time he can't stop himself. He interrupts Gene. "Don't tell me," he says, "that I am going to have to sit here and listen to you for the next nine hundred years."

Gene loves free things. As a promotional gimmick they were giving away root beer with a fill-up at Husky a while back. Gene would get his old truck filled, grab his root beer, drive home and siphon most of the gas into a barrel, maybe throw up, and go back for more.

One day Gene wants a felt pen to take home. Who knows why. But he goes down to the press, where Dave works, and he asks Dave to steal a felt pen for him. Here he is, making twenty dollars an hour, and too cheap to buy a felt pen. Anyway, Dave looks at Gene, and suddenly sees an opportunity. He puts a felt pen down on the bench right in front of Gene, and says, "Steal it yourself." Gene almost did it, Dave told us later. See, Dave figured if Gene took that pen, he could report it. Stealing is one of the things that gets a guy fired, pronto. Gene must have been tempted by that free pen, but he was a little bit too leery to steal it himself.

♦ ♦ ♦

Dave works the press. After eight years he bid for this job, because he'd figured out that it was better than most in the mill. No dust, he stays dry, and he can listen to the radio.

He also gets a helper, to lay out the nylon sling covers, help staple them on, and to stack blocks. Sometimes the helper is me.

Dave's biggest problem, or the one he talks most about, is that his kid wants to be a goalie. Part of this problem is the cost. After buying skates, pads, a mask, a blocker and a stick, there'll be little change left from two grand. But the heart of the problem is that Dave doesn't want his kid to play goal. He can't see him as a goalie. He sees him as a centre, or at least a winger—the kid can skate.

Years ago Dave played two seasons for the New Westminster Bruins. Several of his teammates were drafted to the NHL. Dave wasn't. He came home to Williams Lake and got a job in the sawmill.

Now his kid is twelve. There is a song, a former hit which still plays regularly on Cariboo Radio, and it goes: "My boy's gonna play in the Big League!" Dave always turns that song up. Cody, his boy, loves hockey too, as long as he can play goal. He shows no interest in any other position. This is a real dilemma for Dave.

Otherwise Dave is doing all right. He's still married. They've got a nice house over in Russet Bluff Estates. His wife works at the Royal Bank. Her mother lives with them, which is great. Granny Kate takes care of the kids while Dave and Susan are at work. What's more, she's a hockey fan.

On Saturday evenings Cody and Granny and Dave take their supper down to the family room to watch the game. Dave is a diehard Canucks fan, though they have never won the Cup. Once upon a time Granny had quite a crush on Rocket Richard, and she has supported the Habs ever since. She also loves the Grecian Formula commercials. Cody holds no allegiance to any one team, but to all goalies. He bucks the current trend and favours low scoring games.

Like most of us, Dave does not like his job at the sawmill. He often says he *hates* it. He hurls that word out. Especially when the bander screws up and Dave gets about ten loads behind.

So, one shift, he simply quits. Doesn't make a fuss, or tell anybody, just grabs his lunchkit and walks out to the parking lot.

His helper comes into the press room after piling a rackful of blocks out back and wonders where the hell Dave has got to.

Dave gets into his car. He decides to have one cigarette before leaving the mill for the last time. Before the smoke is finished he is worried about his next mortgage payment, plus what Susan and Granny and Cody will think. So he goes back to work.

Meanwhile I have no clue where Dave has gone. Santok, the stacker operator, he's yelling at me, waving his arms. The foreman, and Warren the forklift driver, they're both on the radio wanting to know what the hold up is. But I'm not trained on the press. What am I supposed to do? I frantically shrug my shoulders at Santok, he turns away in disgust.

"Where have you been?!" I ask Dave when he finally shows up. He can see I'm in a panic, but just waves my question off.

Later on things slow down, we are both sitting there, listening to the radio.

Dave laughs and tells me then how he quit, went out to the parking lot, had that smoke.

All of a sudden though, he turns very serious and looks at me, "Don't tell nobody eh?"

♦ ♦ ♦

Chris is on call. I got this job by accident, honest. A sawmill is the next to last place I ever imagined myself. The mill is lit by tubular white fluorescent lights. In the glare, wearing a hardhat, safety glasses and earplugs, I feel weirdly isolated. My thoughts dart about as if in an aquarium. I catch myself laughing, then glance around to check if anyone has seen me. A few times I've caught other men grinning to themselves.

Haven't decided yet if it is against my principles to be working here, in a sawmill. I put off this decision because I'm making eighteen dollars an hour, and right now I can't turn that down. I do recycle. I'm concerned about pollution, and clearcuts. But I don't talk about this at the mill because I could get beat up. Many of the guys are scared about losing their jobs. They're concerned about their families. It's in their faces, in their expressions when they talk during our breaks. Myself, I can't wait to get out of this job, one way or another. I say nothing.

At first I stack trim-blocks off the chipper conveyor. This is the most recycling-type job in the mill, which makes it easier for me to rationalize. Later I am trained to stack strips, then to stack blocks down at the press. On dayshift I'm generally stacking wood in some form.

I also work graveyard cleanup. There is a giant chain-conveyor which runs through the middle of the sawmill. Its links are bigger than my boots. In the basement, it clanks on and on in the gloom, largely concealed by a lot of other machinery. Great piles of sawdust accumulate, and it is my job to get rid of them. Like a great intestine, the conveyor carries this refuse to an outside dump; during the worst shifts I see myself as a parasite attached to this damned host. As I shovel in the darkness beside the main conveyor, I am lodged in the very gut of madness.

◆ ◆ ◆

Warren drives forklift. Gene rotates. Dave works the press. Chris stacks blocks.

Spring has arrived. The reeds are greening at the end of the lake. The rust-rock bluff above town is studded with blue sage.

In recent weeks the guys have noticed a red fox around the parking lot. Most mornings she sits watchfully at the top of a log pile. They figure it is a female, and that she must have kits in a den nearby.

"I'm gonna trap that fox," says Gene one day at coffee-break.

"Jeezuzchrist," somebody mutters. Dull silence hangs for a moment. Then talk turns to the NHL playoffs. No one believes that Gene means it.

"I set four traps this morning," declares Gene at lunch the next day.

Dave rises half out of his chair, and slowly says, "Are you serious?"

"Yeah," says Gene.

"YOU FUCKIN'—" Dave dives across the table at Gene.

Jas and Rick both grab Dave and pull him back. Fighting is another thing that gets you fired, pronto.

Half the guys in the lunchroom are on their feet now. Gene sits still, a bit pale, puzzled. He just doesn't get it.

Outside there comes a terrific roar as Warren wheels up in the big yellow forklift. He opens his door and flings some things out behind him onto the gravel. Then he revs up the machine, slams it into gear. It charges back and forth, grinds the objects into the gravel. Turns out Warren spotted Gene setting the traps. A few minutes afterward he went along behind and collected them.

Warren climbs down out of his forklift, picks up the tangle of jagged steel, and brings it into the lunchroom. He strides over and drops the mess on the table in front of Gene. One of the ruined traps clatters onto the floor.

Warren doesn't say a word. Just glares, turns around, goes back out and sits inside his forklift, to calm down and eat his sandwiches in peace.

HORSESHOES

The old shoes are rusted. Their orange skin rubs off in our hands as we pick them up. My fingers mark the thick curved heel, darken the metal, make the raised letters more visible: *$2^{1/2}$ lb. drop forged steel*. A big *A* is stamped into the hooked toes of my pair. I lean down, wipe my stained hands in the grass, then on my jeans.

Greg throws the horseshoes with ease. He's big enough to hang a licking on a bear with a hockey stick. No lie, I saw him do it. Years ago when it happened I was all set to shoot that same nuisance bear, had it in my sights, when Greg hollered, " *No Myles, don't!*" He ran out, whacked that brute across the snout, and saved its life. Bear never came back.

Now here we are after supper at the old man's sixtieth birthday/retirement party, for which Greg and his family made the trip especially, up from Vancouver. Dad stood up first from the table, declared by god he had to mow the lawn. The two of us were then tricked into a game of horseshoes so Mom and the women could talk in peace. The old man is already putt-putting around the large front yard in his straw cowboy hat on the shiny new red tractor mower we gave him today, a long necked beer on the seat jutting up between his legs.

Muggy this evening. It smells of reeds from the lake at the lawn's edge, charcoal, burnt barbecue grills, ripeness of fresh cut grass.

Greg's shoe circles through the air, thuds in the sand near enough for one point. Style-wise he's got it wrong. By sheer, unexplainable luck his second shoe lands on top of the first, bounces up against the peg for a leaner, worth two. In a few minutes he's up seven to zip. Game's to twenty-one. Occurs to me that I'm getting beat. Next turn he throws a ringer.

I sip my beer and chuckle, "You're a natural horseshoe man, Gregory. I'll be damned."

"Probably you will," he says, with no trace of a smile. He's a bit pissed off at me, as usual. Greg is drinking cranberry juice, spiked with soda.

Greg has two university degrees, Physical Education, more Physiowhatever, working on a third one, a doctorate he says. He was assistant trainer for the BC Lions one season, his heart runs 52 beats/minute, and he's got a brown belt in Tai Chi. His wife, Jill McFee-Norgaard, is a lawyer. They have a three year old boy, named Justin, and Jill is pregnant again. Or, as she says, " *We* are

24

pregnant." That one cracked me up, must admit. I burst out laughing at supper and caught a serious glare from Greg. My girlfriend Tracy found it funny too, and I noticed the old man with a napkin trying to wipe off his grin. Jill M-N is not a bad looking woman, not at all, but she's too smart for my taste. Anyway, they've got the latest in sandals, kayaks, the Isuzu wagon, whole kit and caboodle.

I throw my horseshoes. First one lands about ten feet left of the pit. Second lands sideways, rolls off runaway like a tire and disappears in the weeds.

"Nice throw," says Greg. "Have another beer." He strolls in his canvas shorts toward the peg to collect his three points. I take a swig, set my bottle on top of the fence post.

I went to college too, for four months. Figured that was enough. Took my second term savings and went to Oahu, had a riot, fried in the sun, lost two teeth when my surfboard slammed me in the face. Then I came home, got married, took a job. I own a house trailer on six acres out the Horsefly Road, a pickup, and a deluxe red and chrome 1969 Norton Commando motorcycle. I drive skidder in the bush, for Lignum Ltd., for the time being, expect to be laid off permanent before too long. The wife left me after three years, but she still gets her share of my pay cheque. I've been working fairly steady upwards of ten years now, and I could use a holiday. Might just take a ride down to Baja. You can wade out and pick your own lobsters there apparently. But no more surfing for me, I learned that lesson.

Greg inspects his shoes in the pit. Picks them up slow and bangs them together, knocks the sand off with a clang.

The old man is down putt-putting along the lake's edge. There's something about a summer evening in the Cariboo, scent of cut grass, icy touch of a bottle, that makes my blood hum in precious peace. Unfortunately Greg is clearly intent on whipping my ass at horseshoes. I've never been much of a competitive athlete type, but I'm also no pervert turned on by humiliation, and horseshoes is one game I know something about. So fine, we'll play.

"What's the score anyway?"

"Eleven to zero, I believe."

"Enough of a handicap then? Time for me to get serious?"

Greg actually chuckles at this. But his voice has an edge to it.

Sun streaks the aspens. Lake is flat as glass but murky, marshy, water almost warm. Its reedy smell mixes with that of the mown lawn. The old man ran an auto parts store for twenty-seven years. He made some money. Our family moved to this lakefront acreage while Greg and I were in high school.

He's just scored, which means I throw first.

I hold the shoe still in both hands, out in front of my belt, squint my eyes at the far peg, then take half a step with my left foot, drop my right knee, swing my right arm. Shoe falls a bit short, toe first. On the second throw I use a bit more force, lightly brush the clip with my thumb, so the shoe slowly flips one full rotation in the air, opens toward the peg, lands within six inches, good for a point. I wipe my hands on my jeans. Take a sip of my beer.

Greg pretends nothing's happened. But he overthrows both his shoes.

We throw the shoes again. This time both of us land one within a finger of the peg, side by side, so the points cancel out.

The old man worked six days a week for as long as I can remember. Chances are Mom and us boys would've eaten supper already by the time he got home. Then he'd have a couple of drinks, sit down to watch TV, doze off in his recliner. Until his stroke last year. But damned if he didn't go back to work as soon as he could get around with a cane, causing Mom no end of grief. Finally, Mom and his business partner got together in secret to launch a sly campaign of suggestions, travel brochures, new golf clubs, until the old man thinks it's his own brilliant idea to retire five years early. Now he likes to say he's *financially independent*, proud as a half-bald rooster.

Sharp clank muffled by sand. No mistake, it's my first ringer.

"Hot damn," I nod.

"Fluke," Greg mutters, shakes his head. This comeback has him rattled.

With much concentration we throw the shoes back and forth. Our eyes follow the path of each through the air, guessing its worth a second before it lands. For every point Greg gains now, I manage to score two or three. He doesn't like it. I see him trying hard not to react, and scratch at my nose to hide my grin.

He never chewed his food too fast, never liked to drink, or scrap. As a teenager guys tended to pick on him at school, after they learned he'd back away. This pumped them up. What they didn't know was that it was his own strength that scared him —he knew what he could do.

At heart Greg is a contender, and he'll surprise you. One year at the Stampede I got a bit too drunk at the beer garden, started bad mouthing some baseball players from out of town. They just grinned and bantered back at first. What made me tip their table over I can't recall, nor do I honestly remember much of what followed. However, there were about two hundred bystanders and they've all told the story over the years, often enough that it's become something of a local tale. Those ball players came out from under that table like hornets from a nest. Apparently I found this very funny until three of them tackled me. Greg chanced to arrive about the time I went under. He was star batter for the local ball team, come to have a friendly beer after the game. He let out a warning yell, then waded in swinging, knocking heads together, and ball players fell like ten pins. After about forty seconds of pretty furious action, a well-meaning woman marches out of the crowd and up to Greg, and yells, " *Stop picking on these guys!* " That's my little brother. He didn't hardly speak to me for a month.

Score is eighteen-thirteen, when I throw another ringer, bringing me within three points. Either of us is able to end the game in one turn.

"Hot damn, hooooeee, ladies and gentlemen the long shot from Horsefly, British Columbia, Mister Myles Norgaard, up and coming World Champion! *Hooo Areeeba!* " and I take a drink, do a little one man samba dance, barechested in boots and jeans.

"Shit," Greg mutters, and shakes his head disgustedly.

I'm two years older than Greg, though the difference looks more like ten. Self-abuse. I'm thirty-one. I've lived maybe half my life, maybe more. Could be next week my skidder will roll on me. Or I bumble on, reach 60 or 66, and I suffer a stroke.

Greg does some breathing exercises. Squats down, extends his arms straight out from his shoulders, then slowly brings each behind his back, until he can clasp his hands.

"Okay, Grasshopper," I say, "let's get on with it."

He stands, but doesn't look at me. He picks up his horseshoes and knocks them together.

Again that soft clang. Greg sets one shoe back down on the ground off to one side. He balances himself, staring at the far peg. He's a big man, but moves gently. He holds the shoe wrong, as I've pointed out. But he throws it so carefully, like it's a matter of life and death. And it hits the peg. Toe first. One point. The second shoe hits the other, but we can't tell for sure if it scored. So he's got nineteen or twenty points.

I'm at fifteen still. All or nothing. My first throw is a touch too hard. Next one's another ringer. Surprises me, and I don't say a thing. My heart thumps like a worn piston.

Greg has his mouth clenched. His last shoe did not score. So he's sitting at nineteen. I'm at eighteen and can take it with a ringer.

With a painful amount of concentration Greg throws his first shoe. Lands short. He steps away from the pit for a minute, wipes his face with his hand. This leaves a slight streak of clownish orange across his forehead, which I choose not to bring to his attention. He takes another deep breath, and steps back in place. Throws the shoe. It bounces off the first, up against the peg for a leaner. Worth two.

"Yes," he whispers.

That's his only reaction. This means he's won the game unless I knock him out of there, or throw a ringer.

I drain the last bit of my beer, which tastes flat. I hitch up the belt on my jeans and step into the pit. For a moment I hold the two shoes linked together, the lower one swinging. I feel the weight of it. Then I set one down, prepare to throw the other. My first throw does the tire trick again, wheels off into the weeds.

"Ah shit," I whine. "Can I have that one over again, Gregory?" His face is blank. He says to me: "Just throw."

Can't help but grin at him.

My second shoe loops slowly through the air, so simply, but trailing so much. It looks good. But it's a half inch too far, toe bangs the peg, thing twirls, catches sunlight and a last instant's hope, then it bounces well left of the pit.

Greg jumps straight up in the air, like a kid half his age, "Yes!" Then he composes himself, slightly embarrassed.

Only for a second I'm disappointed. Then I'm laughing.

He smiles, finally, even chuckles goodheartedly.

"Had you worried eh? Didn't I?"

"Are you joking? No way," he says, laughing outright at his own denial. We're both glad the goddamn game is over.

The old man shuts down the lawn tractor. The quiet surprises us. We both turn and watch him climb out of the seat. He stands there at a distance, a bit off-kilter as he does since the stroke, admiring his shiny new red machine. We head toward him, slowly.

Other sounds drift through the evening now, the bass echo of Mom's country music from inside the house, out on the lake a speedboat humming by, with someone water-skiing. Side by side, we walk across the cut grass.

As we walk Greg quietly clears his throat, then hesitates. I glance at him.

"Jill and I were thinking of staying a few days," he says, "and I was wondering maybe, if there's time, if we could go fishing out west?"

"Fishing?"

"Yeah, you know," he says quickly, awkward, "with a pole and a line, and a tiny hook at the end of the line... to catch fish."

I smile at his effort. He might be a professor, but he's no screamin' hell of a comedian.

"You mean the whole family like, Jill and the boy?"

"No, just you and me, is what I had in mind."

"Well, I don't know... " I say. "I'm working day-shift Monday. It'd have to be tomorrow."

"Tomorrow's fine," he says. "Get an early start, maybe head out to the Chilcotin junction?"

We continue, a few steps in silence through the grass.

"Was this another one of Mom's ideas?" I ask him.

"No," he says, with a sheepish grin. "I thought this one up on my own."

"We'll take a couple jars of cranberry juice I guess?"

"Whatever, please yourself."

"I still don't know Gregory. I just don't know if we should."

"Why not Myles?" he says, so earnest and concerned like, I can hardly keep a straight face.

"Well, in this hot weather, with you being pregnant and all —"

"ARRR!" With one swipe he knocks me down, then stands over top of me trying to push my face in the moist cut grass. I grab his foot, throw him off balance. I'm crawling, scrambling away, he grabs at my foot, yanks my boot off.

The women—Mom, Tracy, and Jill—come out onto the verandah.

Jill M-N inquires, in her nice legal voice, "Who won the match?"

"Me, of course!" I holler back, grinning up at her, "And your man's a sore loser."

Greg says nothing, only narrows his eyes when I glance over. For an odd second I feel the weight of the two steel shoes linked together again, one still in the hand, one swinging.

COME EVENING

The fire's sputter wakes her. Lying still, Shirley's gaze glides through the mare's tail grass, willows, reeds. Curls of mist rise from the slough, the stream, meet flat white sky. Ten steps away, in the littered heart of the camp, the fire livens. She's thirsty. She pushes aside her burlap quilt and searches with her hands, finds the plastic pop bottle, a bit of water cooled by night. This soothes her dry throat as she sips, swallows.

Jim squats by the fire. His fingers feed sticks and coloured scraps of paper into flames which spit and crackle at the edge of a wider mound of ash, greyish cans and broken glass. He does not look up when Shirley appears. Two others are asleep nearby.

"Seen Isaac?"

Jim gives no answer, stares at his fire. Shirley steps closer and swings her foot at him, awkwardly. He pushes her away.

"Go on, fuck off," he grunts.

"Seen Isaac?"

"No!"

As she climbs the hill the lake comes into view, calm, bluer than usual. When the park was made they filled in half the slough with gravel, changed the stream. Used to be the town pumped sewage into it. Signs along this road point to the Bird Sanctuary, and the parking lot. The camp is well hidden, further back in the brush.

Shirley crosses the highway to the *Trading Post*. A high pitched beep sounds as she pushes open the glass door.

The clerk sits behind the till, smoking, leafing through a magazine. He gives Shirley a glance.

Shirley goes to the side counter. There's a coffee pot, a microwave, snack foods and some homemade baking in clear wrap. She looks at these while she slips a handful of sugar packets and creamers into her coat. She lingers, peeking over her shoulder.

The clerk stands up, watching her.

She picks a homemade cheese biscuit and takes it to the counter.

"Eighty-five cents," the clerk says. He sighs, exhales through his nose, while Shirley puts the change down, coin by coin.

Shirley eyes a garbage can outside, almost empty. She slides the contents back into the can and stuffs the bag in the other pocket of her soiled red ski coat. Walking away, she tears open a sugar packet and tips it into her mouth.

◆ ◆ ◆

Shirley walks back down the hill, past the trail to the camp. Jim will still be there, sitting by the fire.

She peers into the ditch as she walks further along the gravel shoulder. Highway 20 crosses the sluggish stream, the BCR tracks, then rises steadily for miles, runs west a day's drive to Bella Coola.

She spots a can. Her steps mark the embankment. She stoops, fishes the can out of the grass, drains a bit of beer out, drops it in the bag. Another one only a few steps further. She works her way along, up the hill, reading the ditch. Shiny cars pass, families on their way to church, dressed up children in the back seats. They pass by her again, an hour and twenty minutes later, rushing home.

Shirley sucks more sugar and follows the roses, spiny sage, rain soaked papers, condoms and liquor bottles flung in the ditch. Past the rodeo arena, the mill yards, the golf course, up the hill.

Past the last town roads, when the cans have thinned out, she rests in the shade of an aspen grove. She eats the biscuit and peels open the creamers, holds the milk in her mouth, lets it seep inside. In a nest of blue grass she naps a while.

◆ ◆ ◆

At *The Lakeview Hotel Beer and Wine Store*, there's a sign taped inside the glass door, facing outward, hand printed by the manager in felt pen: *we take only TWO doz. returns/customer!* This is meant to discourage the troopers, the winos.

But Lorna, the woman who works in the place on Sunday afternoons, takes whatever Shirley brings, as long as Shirley waits outside until there's no one else in the store.

"Otherwise I get in trouble, you see. I can't afford to get in trouble."

Shirley understands. Together they pull the cans out of her plastic bag, fill the cardboard flats of twenty-four, two full plus a few extra cans today, at ten cents each.

Afterward she walks around to the backdoor of the hotel, makes her way through the dim hall into the bar. *The Lakeview* is old, worn. It offers no view of the lake. But the bar remains the largest in town, some summer nights the big room still overflows. This Sunday afternoon it's empty, almost. McNaird and another old cowboy are there, which is no surprise. They fix their eyes on Shirley. As she passes their table McNaird picks up a couple of bills, rubs them together between his thumb and finger, grins at her.

"Shirley, how 'bout it?" he winks at his buddy.

She walks by, gives no response. This irks McNaird.

"Come on Shirl', for old times sake," he calls after her. "Who are you anyhow?"

Shirley takes a seat on the far side of the bar. She drinks a glass of draft and watches the big TV screen on the wall, country music videos. She's aware of the two men watching her. The bartender ignores them all, slouched on a stool with his chin in his hand, staring up at the big screen. The videos all end tenderly, in colour.

A bit later McNaird and his buddy stand up, steady themselves, head for the door. As they're about to pass by Shirley, McNaird pauses, plants his hands on the scarred table, leans close, pushing her back with his sour breath.

"Hey Shirley... I think I seen Isaac the other day."

She studies the old man's lined face, murky eyes.

Maybe he means it, for a moment she can't help but hope.

He laughs, slaps the table, turns away, sunlight cutting into the bar through the double front doors as they leave.

◆ ◆ ◆

Shirley makes her way up the sidewalk, under the hanging white sky. Passing a car dealership she spots half a cigarette on the clean black lot. She smokes it, standing between two rows of shiny new Fords. Out front of the lot is parked a covered wagon, the canvas printed with a big sales ad.

She recalls her first trip to Williams Lake as a girl, with her family in a wagon pulled by horses, coming for the rodeo. So her father could ride in the mountain race. There was a big camp, maybe fifty tents pitched on the green flat alongside the stream.

Isaac always wanted a new car —a Ford. That meant something to him. Once he even walked into the dealer's showroom. Shirley had waited at the door. After a short time the salesman had told them to leave, waved his arm, like she knew he would. Isaac left the showroom, sat down outside on the steps and wouldn't budge. The Ford salesman had phoned the RCMP.

She walks on through town, toward the park behind the mall. There, she sits in the grass with her back against a tree. For a while she stares at the long, two-story concrete building, and the empty parking lot. They've put up a new sign, big orange neon: *Boitanio Mall*.

A few crows fly lazily toward the lake, as they do come evening. Her fingers nest in the green park grass.

Last winter was cold. When trucks geared down, approaching the highway junction, diesel groans echoed in the barren bowl of the rodeo grounds. Thick trails of white exhaust hung in the town streets. Schools and mills shut down for most of a week. Frost-bearded horses stared over barbed wire.

Boitanio Mall management complained of a problem. There were too many people hanging around inside the mall, and no means to buy anything. A bunch of winos, troopers, just in there trying not to freeze. No good for business. Posters went up, threats against loiterers, though everyone knew pressing charges would be too much trouble. Instead, management hired two men, outfitted them with uniforms and a video camera. They patrolled the mall, confronted the troopers, intimidated them.

Mirrors line the walls inside the mall. Shirley had seen herself as the camera followed, her head and hands and feet. She felt overly large. The rest of her body was eaten away, seemed like. Isaac beside her, pretended he was a movie star among the shoppers, in the bright lit stores, full of clothes and furniture and videos.

◆ ◆ ◆

Tonight there is no moon, just the faintest light on the slough, as the stream finds its way. Mosquitoes, and the still flush of marsh smells, water grown over green, wild onion, mint and woody roots, willow smoke.

Jim and Walt sit in the weakening flicker of embers with a bottle. Jim follows her by the whisper of grass against her pants.

She kneels down, sits on her calves.

Walt passes her the bottle. Jim grunts, motions for it with his hand. She takes a quick sip anyway, before giving it to him. The sharp sweet taste so much a part of the camp, the night, the slough, as if the wine comes from the grassy stream itself.

"Seen Isaac?" she asks Walt.

He shakes his head without looking at her.

"No," Jim starts, rises into a crouch. "Don't fuckin' talk no more about Isaac. Hear me? "He raises his arm, bottle in his hand, and thrusts it toward her. "Hear me?!"

Shirley stares at him.

He gestures with the bottle once more, then sits back down, drinking the last of the wine.

When the fire's warmth has passed Shirley makes her way to her bed in the trees.

SCOUT ISLAND

Secure in his office, Rodney Owen is concluding a telephone call. He extends best wishes to the business man in Florida, and offers a suggestion — what about a goose hunt come fall? Rodney sets down the receiver. From the bottom drawer of his desk he pulls out a bottle of Glenfiddich, and pours himself a two-finger drink. A reward.

Rodney Owen knows he is the leading realtor in town. He's largely responsible for an unwritten agreement among his colleagues to keep property values a margin higher than they should be. The bottom is bound to drop out of the local economy, probably within five years. Millworkers into long-term mortgages will be out of luck. Serious buyers, whom Rodney deals with personally, tend to be from Germany or the States, people that aren't bothered by price.

♦ ♦ ♦

Rodney invited several couples over for Paulette's birthday dinner party that night, had it catered by Yee's Restaurant. Paulette knew that Rodney resented giving money to "the Chinaman," because Jim Yee is one of the few local men wealthier than Rodney himself. Of course, it didn't hurt to stay on good terms with Yee, and his restaurant does have the best smorgasbord in town.

After the meal, the men moved out onto the patio, lit cigarettes, and Rodney made the rounds with a bottle of Remy Martin. He swaggered, which made Paulette suspicious. There had been more than the usual tension between them for months. She believed he was having an affair, and this only made her wonder if the woman might even be one of the smiling dinner guests.

This was the first party in their new house, a large, pastel painted split-level, located on an acre lot overlooking the golf course. Paulette was about to lead two women on a tour of the upstairs rooms, when Rodney overheard the plan and put a halt to it.

"It's almost nine!" he said, coming through the French doors into the dining room. "Come on outside everybody, time for the birthday surprise!" He circled behind the guests, waved one hand to urge them forward. "Let's go girls."

When he had the audience in position at the edge of the patio, Rodney made a call on his cell phone and a pickup pulling a horse trailer entered their crescent driveway. The mare was unloaded carefully. Her coat shone the colour of honey, and there was a red ribbon in her blonde mane. Her shoulders and flanks were rounded with muscle.

Several of the guests exclaimed how fine looking a horse she was.

"She's a fine lookin' animal," one of the realtors kept saying, "a real fine piece of horseflesh."

Finally everyone looked to Paulette. She smiled, and brought her hands together. "I just don't know what to say. Thank you sweetheart," she said, grasping Rodney's arm and leaning in to give him a kiss.

◆ ◆ ◆

One side of the indoor arena is walled off. A central gate provides access to the stable area, to a long row of rented box-stalls, a tack room, and a tiny, dusty first aid station. Along the other side of the arena are wooden bleachers, unpainted, foot wide planks, with edges rounded by years of use.

On registration evening, Gail stood beside a card table and chatted briefly with some of those who had signed up for her Western Pleasure class. Every few minutes, her tan face turned upward. Her sinuses prickled, as if a summer cold or mild allergy was coming on. On the table top lay a manila envelope containing money, cheques, and creased forms smudged with ink.

Gail straightened the pile of papers and stepped around in front of the table, a signal to be quiet. She was a bit nervous. There were thirteen students, mostly women older than she was, house-wives or school teachers taking the course for an evening out, and then several younger, slimmer teenagers who tended to sulk when criticized. Gail could guess that much. She had taught these classes last summer. As she tried to speak clearly, her voice came out more stern than she intended, and she had to consciously remind herself to smile. She explained the objectives of the course, then, pointing outside, she motioned to where they could park their vehicles and trailers. As she was doing so, a long silvery sedan pulled up to the open gate of the arena and braked, music blaring.

The late-comer swung her legs out of the car. She was wearing tight purple jeans. She coolly strode over to the table and filled in a registration form. Pen in hand, the long nail of her forefinger wiggled its way across the paper like a lively pink snail. She was close enough that Gail, even with prickly sinuses, caught a whiff of rich musk.

Only when the woman lifted her head did Gail recognize her. Gail nodded. Paulette did likewise, though her expression was indifferent.

◆ ◆ ◆

Gail paces an irregular star pattern in the sandy loam, near the centre of the arena, while her eyes follow the horses and student riders as they trot around the oval perimeter and cross over into a large figure eight. She imagines, just for a moment, that all these women's lives and conflicts are intersecting too. Saddles creak, a horse coughs. Some of these riders will never match the potential of their pedigreed Quarter Horses. This comes of having more money than they know what to do with —not a problem Gail relates to very well. Paulette is a case in point. She is short-reining and frustrating the mare again. Gail has talked to her about this. Why, after thirty years, has Paulette suddenly gotten the idea she wants to ride a horse anyway?

This evening there are only a few spectators on hand, most of them children who rarely stay seated long enough to pay attention. With the bleachers almost all to themselves, they enjoy treading back and forth, hopping up and down among the tiers. Two men, fathers of the children, are seated together and engaged in an easygoing, quiet conversation. Occasionally their attention turns to the arena, and to their wives.

Linked in motion, fourteen horses and riders work their way around the arena. Trotting hooves swish through the dry sandy loam, women whisper or cluck to their mounts, horses snort out of effort or impatience. Near the centre of the arena Gail Michaels paces back and forth, calling out her comments to the students.

"Keep your heels down. You want contact here," Gail bends and firmly slaps the inside of her own left calf. "Gentle, but steady. You're communicating by leg pressure as much as by the reins. Okay? Try to keep that in mind."

A hazy moat of dust arises around the oval perimeter.

At the far end of the bleachers, Rodney Owen sits alone, watching. He wears a thin leather jacket, and wire rimmed glasses. His steady gaze is fixed on Paulette, the curve of her back, and on the golden flanks of the twenty-one thousand dollar palomino.

Unnoticed, high among the rafters of the arena, cry a pair of swallows. Their mud nest has fallen. Only a greyish splotch marks the crossbeam where it was attached. The birds' breasts are the colour of tarnished brass, and their blue, frantic wings create a whorl of dust, that grows to envelope them.

◆ ◆ ◆

At the next class Paulette continues to struggle. Her palomino is the most athletic horse in the entire group, and well trained by a previous handler, but Paulette's inability is provoking the young mare into a lather.

Trotting back and forth, four feet from the arena wall, the students work on full turns. It is a simple exercise meant to link the movements of rider and horse, to minimize the use of reins and bit. They halt, rein lightly, and at the same time the women shift their legs, turn their horses head for tail along the wall.

Near the end of the lesson Paulette's horse finally balks. She tries to yank it around—slaps the ends of the reins against the horse's neck. The mare whirls, lunges against the wall, scraping her shoulder, and the woman's leg. Paulette shouts. She's thrown from the saddle. The palomino dances sideways, fearful, reins dangling between its front hooves. Several women rush to Paulette and with help she gets to her feet, then leans against the wall clutching her knee.

Having decided that Paulette has all the attention she needs, Gail follows the frightened mare. With every step Gail swears under her breath. It is obvious that she should've intervened earlier.

Over her shoulder she nods at one of the other students who has volunteered to drive Paulette to the hospital. The rest of the class is dismissed with a wave.

The mare's skin is torn at the point of her shoulder. Along a narrow cut, the flesh shines red against the matted hair, a steady trickle of blood drips down the golden leg. She limps as Gail leads her to the stable, into the Owen's rented box stall. Whispering soothing words to the horse, Gail strips off the saddle and bridle. It is tooled russet leather, expensive gear. She brushes the mare down, then fetches a sponge and bucket of water. She gently washes the cut. The muscle is already swollen. It will probably scar. She sponges the shoulder, and bending down she wipes the darkly streaked leg. The horse quivers. Gail wrings out the sponge and applies it to the cut, maintaining pressure with her hand, and talking calmly to the mare for a while.

Other horses lean their heads out from stalls along the stable's centre alley. Evening light and silence fans inward from the entrance, although Gail can hear the odd vehicle passing by out on the highway.

Rodney Owen arrives within half an hour. The mare sees him first. Gail turns her head, startled slightly by the man's approach.

He has neat grey hair, wears a thin leather jacket and wire rimmed glasses. She wonders whether he's already been to the hospital, or has come first to see his mare? For an uneasy length of time he stands perfectly still, looking over the door of the box stall.

◆ ◆ ◆

Pulling into her driveway, her rusty Toyota pickup straddles a low hummock thick with dandelions. Gail turns off the key, and the engine's silence prompts her own sigh. She sits still for a moment. Through the open window she looks across the road, over the slough of reeds, beyond the island park to the lake where dusk rolls in like a single wave. Over the industrial services strip, across the green slough, swallows soar and arc upwards into the murky solution of neon and fading daylight.

"Mom?! Can we have shrimp chow mein for Lena's party?" Ricky's outburst comes before she has even shut the back door.

"Can't you say hello at least?"

"Hello," he says, to oblige her, then more eagerly, freckled face beaming, "So can we have chow mein, with shrimps?"

"Let's wait and see," Gail says tactfully, as she sits in a kitchen chair to pull off her boots. The party itself is taken for granted she gathers.

"Aww Mom!"

"Ricky," she replies, in a tone that checks his whining. He pulls a long face, drops his shoulders and plods into the front room.

Submerged in her armchair Lena dozes, dreaming, six feet from the screen of the blaring TV. If anyone were to touch the set, Gail knows she would snap-to, muttering.

Gail's mother had suggested she and Ricky move in, because she was concerned about her Aunt Lena living alone. The old woman was defiantly spry, but the house and yard were just too much for her to tend to by herself anymore. In return for the upkeep she would waive the rent. During their first six months Gail considered moving out to escape the TV noise, cigarette smoke, Lena's lottery obsession, decades worth of opinions and her nightly dreams. Re-hashed over every supper.

But this evening, alone at the kitchen table, with a bottle of beer and a container of leftover potato salad, Gail is grateful for some peace and quiet.

After her meal, she starts on the day's accumulated dishes. Dusk has settled in. For a minute she stands still, with her hands in soothing hot water, resting her weight against the counter. She faces her own faint reflection in the partly-misted window over the sink.

♦ ♦ ♦

Lena's dreams recall a solemn parade she witnessed as a girl, a funeral carriage shining, ivory legs of the Lippizzaners and the reigning clatter of their hooves over slate tiled streets; bread lines, slipping forward between the winter skirts of women, boys in uniform, furious clouds of city birds; endless journeys, by ship and by train; confined within the rattling Model A, headed north on an empty, weed-lined road; her husband, her first lost child, the silent vigils by the radio; her house for sale, a picture in the agency flyer; a mid-summer snowfall; her husband stubbornly shaking his head, not a word to offer.

♦ ♦ ♦

The house is one of a few that, over the years, had been encroached upon by development, the highway bypass and feed outlets, tire stores, machinery repair shops. The neighbouring houses are run-down, and the two nearest the bypass have already been sold to a speculator. He approached Lena too, but she didn't allow him any further than the front step, where he'd planted his polished shoe. Along the short, dead-end street, Lena's yard and garden is the only green patch that remains.

Lena and Ricky look after one another on the days that Gail works. Usually after Lena has fueled herself with enough coffee, she and Ricky and the dog walk over to the park on Scout Island.

Scout Island has a low hill of willows and a man-made beach. When the gravel causeway was built to the island and bird sanctuary the lake's natural circulation was cut off; some say this makes the water partially stagnant and murky.

Lena and Ricky and Dusty think of it as their park. The wiry border collie leads the way. Ricky skips and scampers, marches with a reed sword like a little monarch. Lena follows at a distance in her Nike cross-trainers, cigarettes bulging in the pocket of her sweater, and wielding her shiny aluminum cane. She has outlived all expectations. She sits on the picnic bench and watches Ricky, on the swing, pumping himself into the air or racing across the grass after the dog.

That morning Dusty had trotted out of the brush with a well-ripened prize between her teeth. Ricky had chased her until he got ahold of the bone, and into a tussle.

"Put that filthy thing down Ricky, for heaven's sake," Lena had called out to him, rising from her bench. She paused to light a cigarette for the walk home and stuffed the pack in the pocket of her sweater.

Tourists, a couple from Oregon, sat eating their lunch inside their camper van. They watched as Lena, Ricky and Dusty left the park, and made their way home over the causeway.

Being avid birdwatchers, the couple were lured off the highway by signs to the sanctuary. They had spotted a number of ducks, mallards and widgeons, a few white gulls looking out of place on the shore of such an arid landscape, also swallows and red-wing blackbirds. Just before they were about to leave the man took their tuna tin and cucumber peelings over to the garbage can. He spotted the thick, unusual bone lying in the grass nearby. He bent down to examine it. He was a taxidermist in Portland, and he knew this bone wasn't from any animal he had ever worked with. Twenty minutes later, from a service station pay phone, he called the RCMP.

◆ ◆ ◆

The bone was identified as the right tibia of a human. The victim was most likely an adult male, of small stature. Traces of connective tissue adhered to the proximal end, periostium seventy percent intact, post-mortem distal fracture due to a scavenging carnivore. This much was confirmed by Sergeant Clarke of the RCMP, a forensic specialist, who was flown in to assist with the investigation. He took charge of the Scout Island search. Carefully packaged, the tibia was sent south on Air BC's morning flight. From the Vancouver airport it was taken directly to the Provincial Coroner's lab in Burnaby, to undergo closer study and testing, in order to determine the victim's age, race and health history.

◆ ◆ ◆

The police and hounds would search the park and the bird preserve for the next three days. Wearing fluorescent orange windbreakers, the men resembled bright, clumsy birds too large to fly. In hipwaders they slog through the brush and marshland. Startled ducks burst from cover, and streak away over the grey lake.

That afternoon the sky is an eerie expanse of white seamed to the timber and red rock horizon. Stirred by random traffic, dust hangs in the bowl of earth around the town. Windows glint with flat light. Concrete and baked mud resonate heat.

Spidery, uprooted sagebrush skitter along the highway.

Dusty is barking in the front yard. The hounds' calls from Scout Island have upset her. Gail is also on edge. All set to tell the dog to shut up, she flings open the front door.

In the driveway, behind her own pickup, is parked a blue sedan. A man she's never seen before is bent over, with his arms braced against his knees, talking to Ricky. Half-way down the walk Dusty stands and barks, throwing her nose in the air.

"Ricky! Come here —" she's down the steps, rushing out in her sock feet.

Her son turns, wondering what the fuss is all about. The man straightens up. Then he touches the boy's shoulder.

"Right now, Ricky. Come here!" she repeats, and reaches out

to take hold of him, drawing him away from the stranger. "Who are you?" she demands.

The man urges the boy toward his mother, while taking a step backward.

"Please, it's alright," the man stammers, pulling his hands in close to his chest. "I'm with Social Services. My name is Vince Beal. I didn't mean to startle you, I was just asking Ricky if his mother was in, I —"

"I'm his mother," Gail says, trying to calm her voice, an icy tingle in her arms and chest. "What do you want?"

"I believe a woman from our office called you —"

"Yes! But nobody's told me what this is all about. The dog found those goddamn bones, okay," Gail points angrily toward the park. "But what do you people want?"

"We're only concerned about Ricky's well-being Mrs. Langkamer. We received a report that he was in the care of an elderly woman, who claimed to be his guardian. Perhaps there's been a misunderstanding. You are Ricky's legal guardian?"

"I'm his mother, I just told you," Gail says sharply, then takes a deep breath, puts her hand over her mouth for a moment, as if to hold back other words. "Yes, maybe there's been a mix-up. My name is not Langkamer, that's my aunt, actually my great-aunt. My name is Michaels, Gail Michaels. I'm sorry for yelling at you —but this business has gotten on my nerves, with the police, the newspaper and your office calling, and those bloody dogs," she points again toward the park, then her arm falls to her side.

"It's quite understandable," Vince nods his head, attempts a smile. He seems quite harmless now, dressed in a golf shirt, corduroy pants and loafers, nodding his head. Half bald and tired looking, though fairly young, he hunches slightly and gestures toward his briefcase on the hood of the sedan. "And I'm very sorry to trouble you any further. But if I could just get a little bit of information, just to complete this report and be done with it, I'll be on my way. Promise."

"Better do it Mom," Ricky pipes up. She brushes his hair with her fingers, gives him a smile.

"Okay, we may as well go in the house I guess. There's coffee on, if you'd care for a cup?"

"Thank you," he nods, clearly relieved. "That's sounds great. This really won't take long. The police seem to have the wrong impression from Mrs. Langkamer."

"The police? Well," says Gail dryly, picturing Lena's feisty exchange with the officers, "that explains things, to some extent."

"I see," the man nods politely, as he follows Gail up the front steps. He pauses to remove his shoes.

"Oh don't bother about that," she says, then immediately worries what it means, to a social worker, if they wear shoes in the kitchen. She glances over the counters and floor, fearing dirty dishes or a case of beer in sight, but things are in fair order.

She sets out two mugs on the table, gets the milk carton from the fridge, chooses to pour some in a serving pitcher before setting it on the table. Ricky has taken the third chair at the table. While Vince has his head down, digging in his briefcase, Gail gives Ricky a level gaze and nods her head toward the front room. He pretends to miss this signal.

"Can I have a glass of milk Mom?" he says, with unusual politeness.

"Sure you can," she says, and pours it for him, "How 'bout if you take it in the front room, maybe watch TV for a while?"

"Too much garbage on TV, Mom. That's what you always say," Ricky answers, dodging her gaze.

"Well then, why don't you go out back, and give Lena some help in the garden?"

Ricky considers this. "Okay, I'll just finish my milk first."

Gail pours coffee in the mugs, and prepares to lay down the law.

"Thanks very much," says Vince, and he nods at Gail, meaning it's fine if the boy stays.

Vince explains the Ministry's obligation to look into every report submitted to their office. Normally the source is kept confidential, but Vince had already let it slip about the police. According to them, Mrs. Langkamer had claimed to be Ricky's guardian. Due to her age, the police were somewhat concerned about the boy's welfare, and had notified Social Services.

Vince asks a few related questions, apologetically, Gail is reassured that he's satisfied by her answers. Ricky slowly sips his milk. Vince makes a few notes on a form, then slips it into his case; he snaps the case shut, and sets it off to one side of his chair.

"I wish every call were that simple," he says.

Gail returns the man's smile. Ricky launches into conversation with Vince, who is patient, and good natured, but declines a second cup of coffee. As he stands to leave, he looks out the kitchen window, watching the orange windbreakers of the policemen over at the park.

"Have they found anything?" she asks. "Have you heard?"

"Apparently not. Different rumours are going around, but no one knows anything for sure. The police have files on several missing persons. Maybe one of them went through the ice last fall," Vince says.

Gail turns away from the window.

"Today is supposed to be the last day of the search."

"Thank god for that," she says, almost in a whisper.

Vince nods solemnly, "I suppose it hasn't been very pleasant, having to watch them."

"It's been fun!" Ricky protests.

This remark catches both adults off-guard. Vince gives a well-meaning smile, and reaches for the door.

Near the bottom of the front steps Lena Langkamer stands with her hoe. Under the brunt of Lena's stare, Vince starts to measure his steps sideways, calculating the potential arc of that garden tool. She wears Nikes and a baggy brown dress. Garden dust darkens the pattern of wrinkles in her face. Her hair is stiff and wild. Her eyes are pebbles of turquoise washed by ninety-one years, and a smoking cigarette slants from the corner of her lip.

"Hello," Vince smiles, sneaking one foot warily off the walk, attempting to pass by.

The old woman doesn't speak. She takes a step forward, lifts her hoe, whams the metal blade down against the sidewalk concrete. Vince takes a little hop backward, lands with both feet on the lawn, briefcase rising instinctively like a shield. He glances back up at Gail, with a worried grin.

Gail covers her eyes with her hand, peeks through her fingers.

Lena thrusts the handle of the hoe at Vince, tilts her head a bit as she glares. "Are you a real estate man?!" she growls.

"Ah, no, no," Vince laughs anxiously. "No, I have nothing to do with real estate. I promise."

"Lucky for you," says Lena, drawing back her hoe, lifting her chin.

◆ ◆ ◆

Deep in her arm-chair, Lena dreams the police are involved in the scheme to take her house, and that pictures of it have been stapled up all over town. They want the bones too, buried in her garden. Digging the soil with her hand shovel she comes across other bits of the skeleton, the colour of parsnips, but hard, harder even than horseradish tubers. Carefully she covers them up again, almost certain she knows whose bones they are, and feeling honour bound to protect them.

COUNTRY BOYS

September is muggy in this town. In a week or two there will come a morning with a chill and we'll know it is fall. Today, my first day teaching here, I'm sweating. All the windows are open, but there is no breeze. The room faces west, and even through the blinds the afternoon sun makes me squint. It's an old building. I attended this same high school only nine years ago.

Standing by my desk, I read out the list of names and try to fix in memory the faces of the students who answer.

For years I had plotted my escape from this town, over lunch-hours sitting in a booth at the Dairy Queen, moodily sucking a milkshake. Only to come full circle, not unlike a fish, or a bird.

I've discovered that there are several teachers in this district, and two social workers that I know of, who also grew up here. When by chance we meet on the street we seem to speak with wry secrecy. As if none of us know exactly why we're here.

"Amar Singh?"

"Here."

"Jolene Thibeau?"

"Yup."

"Alice Trimmer?"

No one answers.

I look up from my class list, and search the rows. And finally in the rear, near the window, a girl lifts her hand without making a sound. She's quite large, and poorly dressed. I'm inclined to take her silence for shyness. I nod, and smile at her. She does not smile back. She seems alert, yet her eyelids droop partly, her mouth has a sullen sag, her face and posture express belligerence.

Her gaze unnerves me, though I could not say exactly why—until I re-read her family name. I realize she brings someone else to mind.

♦ ♦ ♦

When I was a boy my parents owned a place, six hillside acres and an older house about fifteen kilometres south of town. The year I turned thirteen, and entered junior high, my parents bought a larger, newer home, which was located near the golf course. I divide my memories between boyhood and adolescence according to that move.

The earlier house was in a sparse, rural neighbourhood, where there lived an odd assortment of people. One of the nicer farms was owned by an eccentric retired woman, who was rumoured to have been a doctor. Darryl Trimmer told me that he'd cut her grass a few times, and when it came time to pay him, she had taken the money from a container she kept in her ice box.

The Trimmer family was indisputably strange. They lived in a long, patch-board shack that had originally been built to house turkeys. There were the parents, and seven or eight kids, plus some other adult relation, who was mentally challenged if I remember correctly. They were commonly the subject of gossip or hushed jokes. But if I repeated any of this at home, my mother would reprimand me. She said the Trimmer's situation was "really very sad."

For one or two of those boyhood summers I actually spent time with Darryl, the oldest of the Trimmer kids. He was two or three years older than I was, but was in the same grade, being slowly shuffled through elementary. He weighed two hundred pounds in grade seven. He had thin, oily brown hair, and a whiny voice. And he became the school bully. He was the only kid for miles around that was close to my own age, and being on speaking terms with him made it less likely that he'd beat me up.

One afternoon he stopped by our gate, waved me out to talk with him and let it be known that he'd found the Doctor's missing cow. It was dead. Darryl had a .22 rifle, and he was going out to shoot some holes in the carcass. He said I could come if I wanted.

On one previous safari we had stuffed frogs into milk cartons and then chucked rocks at them, until the cartons got shredded, and numerous limp frogs' bodies floated, pale bellies up, in the murky pond. For days after this slaughter I carried guilt, winced whenever I pictured the dead frogs. Yet a couple of weeks later I went again. That time, from the cover of a willow thicket, we maimed several of the Doctor's chickens with our slingshots. Thoughts of crippled white hens, and Darryl's vicious glee, made me queasy. So when I caught sight of him standing by our gate that afternoon, beckoning me with his fat arm, I tried to come up with any excuse not to go. But he had a bully's love of persuasion. The cow was already dead, he reminded me, what he had in mind was only a bit of target practice. Perhaps the rifle represented an advance in weaponry which intrigued me, albeit a rusty Cooey. Darryl was more than usually excited by his idea. He showed me the half-full box of cartridges as he began walking away, and, with my hands in my blue jeans, I followed him.

We walked along the road for about two kilometres. It skirted the ridge, hugged the fringe of the slough, followed the flattest ground as older country roads tend to do. Near the pond we struck off into the woods, sometimes having to make our way around stretches of mud and cattails. Mosquitoes were thick, and caused a tinge of panic in me. There was no trail. But we were not that far from the road. I knew that the direction we were headed would bring us around back of the Doctor's property, where there was an old Forestry trail that could lead me home.

It occurred to me to wonder how Darryl had discovered the cow. What had he been doing back here in the first place?

He lumbered ahead of me through the willows and thimble-berries. His thick, soft arms bulged out of his t-shirt, and a roll of grey pink flesh showed between the shirt and his enormous farmer pants. With no regard for the rifle, he waved it like a machete at the brush, uttering curses.

The trees were mostly skinny swamp spruce, trailing black moss. They grew thick enough that in the midst of them it became like dusk. What sunlight penetrated fell in sharp-sided shapes among the dark trunks, reeds and ferns. The lush growth fascinated me; the profuse green seemed to swallow us. My mind turned to primitive strategies for survival, trying to recall anything I might have learned on the subject from TV.

It took us thirty or forty minutes to reach the small clearing where the dead cow lay. At last we waded into a putrid, invisible mist which surrounded the clearing. As soon as he saw the cow Darryl began to giggle.

"There!" he pointed, his chuckle thinning to a short shriek, "There's my fuckin' dead cow."

Immediately he threw up the rifle, as if the bloated thing was all set to run away he fired. He worked the bolt and fired again.

The sudden, piercing cracks startled me. I flinched, then crouched down, stock still.

Darryl whirled around laughing, waving the rifle, and was momentarily puzzled. Then he saw me kneeling and realized how frightened I was. He fell silent, except for his wheezing, while a maniacal gleam came into his eyes.

"That's my cow," he said, grinning, with the blue barrel of the gun slanted toward me, "isn't it?"

I did not speak, but nodded.

He then turned, lifted the rifle, fired again, and again.

The cow was mostly white, with reddish freckles, lying on its side with two legs stiff in the air. The belly was swollen at least twice normal size. As Darryl blasted away, dark cords of rotted flesh erupted wildly from behind the neck, and ribs, and flank of the carcass. Even from thirty yards away I could see the flies clustered on the nose and eyes, small black clouds rose with the impact of the bullets, barely dispersed, then returned to their zealous feed. The pressure of its stink was like steam in the clearing, clinging to me where I crouched, watching. Sun beat down, the swamp grass shone unnaturally green. Mosquitoes swarmed nearby, humming in my ears, and I tried desperately not to think about them. The scene before me was repulsive. But I did not turn away.

He moved in closer, to do more damage. He fired, worked the bolt as he took another wheezing clumsy stride, fired again, until he was less than ten steps from the fly covered head. It amazed me that the smell didn't choke him.

Then I saw something.

From where Darryl stood, nearer the head, with his attention focused down the rifle barrel, he missed seeing those first spasms of the cow's belly. That cow started to move.

I opened my mouth to yell and could not.

Now the half-rotted beast's rear leg flexed. It struggled, as if to rise.

Darryl fired again, giggling. Flesh spattered. He'd noticed nothing yet.

Cows get up hind first. Flies lifted in a buzzing cloud. Ragged swamp spruce ringed the clearing, like primitives in a trance. Harsh sun glared down on the grass, and on Darryl, making his sweaty skin shine.

Then he saw it move. He held the rifle aside, in one hand, and his wide grin waned all of a sudden.

The muscles of the cow's flank convulsed, and the stiff, piss-stained tail flipped up.

Darryl stepped backwards, awkwardly reaching out behind him, without taking his eyes off the cow. The rifle barrel slashed the air. The grass was knee-high, and thick. Darryl tripped. The gun fired, its bark tightly muffled.

From between the freckled white hind legs of the cow a black thing emerged. Shapeless at first. It glistened, shrouded with lumps of slime. Then wings appeared, and the head shook, flinging off its crown of clotted blood. It hopped free of the cow's hollow gut. It hopped once more, spread its large wings and loomed upward in the sunlight, veered off right above me, and silently disappeared into the woods.

When I reached Darryl he was lying on his side, breathlessly clutching grass tight in both his fists. The rifle was underneath him.

I touched his shoulder, gently moved him enough to examine his front. I felt older, charged with duty. He wasn't hurt. Only scared.

After Darryl got himself together, I led the way out through the spruce stand to the old Forestry trail. Oddly, we did not speak about the cow or the bird. I had to restrain my urge to break into a run. I knew that I could outrun Darryl, leave him alone in the woods, crying; it would have served him right.

By the shorter route I'd chosen, we reached the gravel road in fifteen or twenty minutes. By then Darryl had regained his composure enough to warn me not to tell anyone where the dead cow was, or anything else.

When I did not respond, he warned me again. I turned and faced him for a moment, met his frantic eyes, and shrugged my shoulders. I turned away toward home, and Darryl trudged off in the other direction.

♦ ♦ ♦

"Mr. Matthews?" a student asks, her eyebrows raised, glancing sideways at her friends.

"Hmm?"

The entire class is watching me, including the Trimmer girl. I have no idea how long I've been standing there.

"Oh, pardon me," I stammer, red-faced. "It's been a long day. Where was I? Curtis Unger?"

"Here, sir."

Trimmer is not such an uncommon name. But this is a small town. Alice must be related to Darryl, perhaps even his youngest sister.

♦ ♦ ♦

From the beginning I did well in junior high. Good marks came easily to me. I got involved in the student newspaper and played for the soccer team. One of the first years, I cannot recall whether it was grade eight or nine, I received an award for being the top student.

My parents had moved to their new home when my father was promoted to management within the Fish and Wildlife Department. He always urged me to concentrate on sciences in school, but my mother encouraged me to follow my own interests, history and English. Both quietly assumed, as I soon did, that I would go on to university. I was growing scornful of the stolid, dusty town we lived in, and was impatient to get away.

I no longer rode the school bus, so whatever link I'd had to Darryl Trimmer was severed. He entered grade eight the same year I did. Now he seemed more of a freak than a bully. Within the first month he was nicknamed "Tubby," "Dumbo," and "Trimmer-than-what?" The latter enraged Darryl. He clumsily charged after those who taunted him, which, if nothing else, provided some lunch-hour entertainment. Darryl began a foolish campaign to discover who had coined the phrase, and swore to get his vengeance. It was just as well for me that he never learned.

Darryl was permanently excused from PE class. Most assumed he was just too fat, but I heard other rumours: that he was actually sexless, or contrarily, that he was growing breasts.

We were together in only one class: Introductory Shop. He had approached me a few times, as if we were friends but I did not respond.

It was still early in the fall, when Darryl was suspended for a week.

We were making pencil trays or bird houses and I was working at a bench at the far end of the shop. A sudden argument flared up between Darryl and Eddy, a smaller kid working next to him, over who got to use the handsaw. After a moment Eddy shrugged, started laughing and turned away, getting in a last quip about "Trimmer-than-what?"

Darryl's arm shot out. With his right hand he grabbed Eddy by the back of the shirt collar, and with his left he grabbed a chisel off the work bench.

"WHAT?!" Darryl screamed into Eddy's ear. He pressed the chisel against his cheek, and choked him with the shirt collar.

The shop went silent, except for the humming of a fan.

Mr. McTavish quickly stepped out of his office but stopped in his tracks when he realized the danger.

From where I was, I saw the colour drain from Eddy's face.

"Darryl!" said Mr. McTavish. Then he paused and swallowed. "Darryl, please put that chisel down."

Darryl responded by tightening his grip on the shirt collar and giving it a yank. Then he smiled.

Eddy's face was creased with terror. Darryl pushed him to the floor, and threw the chisel onto the bench.

Darryl was suspended for a week. Eddy's parents were furious. They went so far as to submit a petition, which many had signed, demanding that Darryl Trimmer be expelled. The town paper came out with an editorial on violence in the high school.

Darryl did return to school, for a month or so, as I remember. Then he was gone again, and there was speculation among the students that he'd been sent away somewhere, or, had chosen to quit.

What he had chosen, as it turned out, was to hang himself.

TASEKO

The rifles, in their leather scabbards, were placed behind the seat of the pickup. The boy's parents were talking quietly on the porch, while he waited with Lars in the truck. He was fidgety. Lars was smoking his pipe. At last his father came down the steps, carrying his hunting boots which shone with dubbin. As they pulled out Mother waved, especially to her boy it seemed. He almost wished she hadn't. Like Lars he simply lifted his hand.

They drove several hours on the highway, tires whining on the dry grey pavement, sunshine glinting on the hood, warm on the dash. The two men spoke about work, which was something only distant to the boy. He listened to them, and to the fading radio, but most of his attention was on the land: growth lines dividing the spruce and aspens, rock ridge colours, cattail ponds and open grassy slopes. West of Lee's Corner was gravel road and dust. They crossed the Chilcotin River, then climbed higher up the Plateau. Now, on the crest of a hill, great reaches of country came into sight, vast dark stands of jackpine, and autumn wild meadows. It was largely untouched, except for occasional corrals or rail fences sketched into the distance.

Lars geared down as they neared a number of plain plywood houses, a few brightly painted. Long-traveled cars were parked under the trees, or already half-buried in the weeds. Children came close to the road to watch them pass. Lars waved and the kids grinned and ran behind the pickup shouting. Past the houses was a pole corral holding a half dozen horses. They were milling about nervously, rolling their eyes, trotting back and forth, kicking up loose dirt. A man stood inside the corral holding an open lariat. He did not turn to the road. The boys, perched on the fence, looked briefly, but then went back to watching the man with the rope and the horses. The boy in the pickup twisted in his seat, gazing back until they had rounded the next bend.

By late afternoon they were into the first folds of the Coast Range, following a river that was glacial green and laced with rapids. The road became two ruts worn in scant mountain turf. Lars pointed out a big blunt peak to the west, called Tatlow, that was sacred to the Tsilhqot'in people.

The men had a site in mind for a camp; from there they could cover two adjoining valleys. They stepped out of the truck into the bite of an icy wind. The boy's fingers numbed as he helped his father assemble their tent. As dusk crept quickly westward, the snow on the peaks and in the facial crevices retained the essence of the day's light.

◆ ◆ ◆

In the morning, frost clustered in the bunchgrass and the juniper needles and clung in webs against the tires and fenders of the truck.

The boy was first up and set to making a fire with dry willow leaves and bone white branches of pine. Then he dug the charred coffee pot out of the campbox and took it down to the creek. Ice was an inch thick at its edge; a narrow stream of dark, quick water. The boy dipped into this, then scooted back to his fire. He sat on his heels with his back to the warmth, hands tucked deep into his coat. A vibrant light rose above the mountains as the pine sticks snapped in the fire.

Lars always hunted alone. This trip he was after a goat, so he worked the higher ridges, sometimes crossing the patches of grainy snow that had lasted through summer at that altitude. He left early each morning, taking only rye bread and cheese for lunch, and did not return until dusk.

The boy and his father stayed below timberline most of the time, watching the game trails and meadows for moose or mule deer. They each carried a small pack for their lunch and a Thermos. On a leather sling over one shoulder his father had an Enfield .303, with a long black scope. It was accurate at three hundred yards or more. The boy carried his own Winchester carbine. He was proud of the gun, careful not to scuff it in the brush, but leery with it too. Lightly he touched the cool lip of the trigger and the knurled steel hammer end. They stopped often, to listen, waiting for movement in the woods.

Scanning, his binoculars in hand, the boy's father would point out their next route. As they ventured higher, crossing the alpine slopes and mossy rock-slides, the tumbled blue puzzle of the Pacific mountains stretched north and south.

Each evening his father and Lars spread the map on the tailgate and described the country they had crossed. Under a kerosene lamp hanging from the truck's canopy the three of them prepared a meal. Afterward they settled close to the fire and Lars poured dark rum into their tea. He lit his pipe with a burning twig. The boy cupped his hands around the hot, scented drink, listening closely to the men's talk and quiet laughter. He was intently aware of when his father spoke. For a moment he did not recognize that voice, and he did not trust his own. Often, as if he heard something, he looked over his shoulder. Just there, beyond the firelight, was the wild, an absolute darkness.

After four days they had seen no game. Any tracks or sign they found seemed to be more than a week old, which puzzled Lars. He had hunted the region for years and had always known it to be rich with wildlife. But each day it grew colder and perhaps the animals had already moved west or south to lower valleys.

Lying in the tent one night, after his father was asleep, the boy heard a low, lasting howl; but the aged wolf may have been calling from the dark slope of a dream.

◆ ◆ ◆

On the morning of the fifth day there was two inches of snow on the ground and the boughs of the pines and grey clouds were banked above the mountains, covering the peaks. Over breakfast they had to make a decision. It was two hours by truck to the good road. If it began to snow again during the day, and continued for any time, they could have real trouble getting out. However, the snow would allow them to finally determine if there was any game around, and if there was, today it could be easily tracked. Lars and the boy looked to his father. He nodded. Lars sorted out his pack and was away within minutes.

It was tough going. The snow on the dried grass made any incline slippery and for the first time the boy had trouble keeping up. His boots chafed him. It was cold and he'd worn extra clothing which now had him sweating. Perhaps his father had wanted to leave that morning; he seemed impatient. He looked gruff with five days of beard.

Not wanting to range too far in the uncertain weather, they checked benches and thickets they had covered on previous days. The boy's father hoped to get a deer. He recalled his own first hunting trip, and he wanted something like that for his son. The boy sensed this. For a time he shared his father's frustration. But later that afternoon when they turned back for camp, the boy felt only relief.

♦ ♦ ♦

A shot ripped the white valley.

When the boy started to speak, to ask —his father sharply raised a hand. The man's attention strained for the direction of the echo.

During those few taut moments —the gun's report gone, snow and wind rising, spirits moaning in the timber —in that time the boy first perceived his own unfolding solitude.

Another shot. Before the sound of the kill was lost his father headed towards it. The boy jogged behind, frightened now by the haste with which they broke through the brush. But it was almost dusk, and his father wanted to find Lars and help him dress the animal. They made a quick stop in camp to gather some rope and an axe. Then they set off for the jutting bluff across the valley.

It was difficult to see the depth of ravines until they had plunged into them. Icy branches clawed at their clothing. Despite the pace their progress seemed slow and stubborn. It took half an hour to reach the base of the rock bluff. Then his father stopped, motioned for the boy to be quiet, and called out to Lars. A shout from behind them startled the boy.

In a few minutes they discovered the hunter in a tiny matted clearing, a moose bed. Lars knelt close to the dead bull. Scarlet gore was smeared the length of his arms and flecks of it were sticking in his beard. Beside him a mass of blue-white guts was steaming. An olid smell made the boy catch his breath. The men were laughing. His father slapped Lars on the shoulder and got blood on his hand.

They cleaned the animal, then doggedly chopped the carcass lengthwise along the spine. His father rigged a rope harness around each half. The sides weighed several hundred pounds, but the hide slid on the snow, and they had to get the meat to camp that night.

The boy looked over at the long head of the moose, propped up by the bloody stump of its neck. Lars took the axe and with a few deft blows severed the rack from the skull. The boy winced at the last stroke, as the blade slit one eye, and with a thick suck the antlers broke loose. Lars held them a moment, and then handed them to the boy. The men took up the ropes on the sides of glistening meat. The boy shouldered the rack and followed them through the darkness.

LET THE DAY PERISH

Let the day perish wherein I was born, and the night in which it was said, There is a man-child conceived.

—Job 3:3

After breakfast Stuart takes his coffee out on the porch for another look at his grain field. The Heeler bitch trots around the corner of the house, then sits with her white eyes on him, her muzzle creased in a smirk.

Stuart is a man of mid-stature, with large features: a fierce nose, full mustache and a serious slope of skull crowned by a Stetson. A beefy paunch presses out the snaps of his shirt, and his jean pantleg is caught atop one boot. The sight of his grain strikes him as peaceful. It's a crop as good as any in the Cariboo have seen before; ninety acres of bright feathered barley and blue stemmed oats, six feet high in some places. Each day for a week he has meant to cut it, and every morning while admiring the stand he has put off the job. In a breeze the barley ripples like the strings of a guitar. It smells green. A man from the *Tribune* came and took a photo of Stuart standing in the field, holding his hat above his head. It is on page three of the last edition; you can hardly see his face in the grain, but he looks proud.

This morning he must swath it; it's plenty ripe and top heavy. A few patches already have laid over. The field is bordered by a thin strip of willow and saskatoon, and then the valley road. Cows and calves appear from out of the brush, trailed by Lyle Keller on his roan mare. He must be moving his sorry little herd to the government pasture.

In the same instant, Stuart remembers his bull and hears its first horny bellow from the barnyard. The old Simmental is by himself in one of the smaller corrals where only a narrow stretch of ground and two tired fences separate him from the road.

Stuart drops his coffee mug and charges directly through Fran's bean patch. Amid his own curses he can hear his son Kevin shout and the sound of pine rails breaking. He reaches the barnyard just as the bull charges into the wire.

Kevin chases the bull as if the Simmental is a pup dog in a scrap and he's going to pull it out by the tail. He's tumbled by a flailing hoof. Three strands of the fence snap, recoil, topple the bull in a snarl of barbed wire. Two strands hold taut and these do the damage. The animal stills for a second, bellows desperately, and Stuart seizes a foreleg. This only triggers fury. The bull rages then falls, exhausted. The hair on his belly is a mat of blood, wire points are embedded in the muscle of his hams.

"Christ!" Stuart gasps as a loop of wire rips his arm. "Your jacket," he yells at Kevin, who then tries to wrap the bull's head.

"Get the cutters from the truck!"

Stuart pulls the jacket over the bull's rolling, fear-veined eyes. When Kevin returns, Stuart grabs the cutters from his hand. He pries angrily at the wires constricting the bull, then yanks the jacket loose and jumps out of the way.

The bull lies there, huffing. Stuart prods it with his boot. The Simmental lurches to his feet and staggers on his first step, drags his left hind leg. Now Stuart sees the mangled sack, a large purple nut distended and bleeding, and as the bull drops, grunting, drooling, the bare testicle lolls in the dust.

Shiny blue flies are drawn to the suffering bull and the blood browning in the yard. Distant cottonwoods are glittering. The Heeler pants noisily. Stuart clenches his teeth, bends to pick up his battered Stetson, and slaps it against his leg as he walks away.

◆ ◆ ◆

Folks in the valley speculated that Stuart had struck a deal with God; this was the only explanation for his unrivaled success as a rancher. Of course he worked hard, watched the market, and was known to be a Mason, but these factors could not account for all his good fortune. Over the years, nourished by whiskey and horseshit, the joke grew into a bit of a story. Once upon a time in Montana, when Stuart was a young cowboy chasing strays, he met up with the Old Man on a sagebrush mesa. In all his glory the Lord

God stood there, in a buffalo coat, Levis, and boots handmade by Mexican angels. They jawed a while —about the recent war, Eisenhower, the weather and the price of beef. And God liked the boy so He made him an offer. He unfurled the hide of a mountain lion, to reveal a contract in holy script, and at the tail end Stuart carved his mark.

◆ ◆ ◆

"What on earth?!" cries Fran when her husband appears in the doorway. She pulls him into a chair, hustles to fill a bowl with warm water, grabs a towel. "Here, take off that shirt," she says and helps peel it from his bulky shoulders. His torso is pale except for his tanned neck and forearms, and the dark silver hair on his chest. "I heard some commotion, Kevin shouting, but I couldn't tell what was going on."

"Ah, Lyle run his goddamn cows down the road 'stead of the river trail," Stuart says. He stomps his boot as Fran dabs the cut with antiseptic. She chides him gently as she wraps the bandage.

She is a thin woman with nervous hands, brittle red hair, and an angular face that has grown severe after many seasons of marriage. Her eyes vary from pale green to hazel, and are often worried. She glances up in time to see Kevin passing furtively by the kitchen window. Fran recognizes the look in her son's eye, but says nothing now to Stuart, whose back is turned. Her hand is resting on his neck and she feels him clear his throat.

"So. We got four thousand bucks worth of hamburger out there in the yard."

"Oh goodness," sighs Fran, dismayed. "Can't we call the vet out anyway? He might fix things, he —"

"That bull," retorts Stuart, "has fixed himself real fine."

Fran pours them coffee. The finish on the table has worn off where their plates are set three times a day. The lazy-susan at the centre carries salt, pepper and steak sauce, various bills wedged in between. Outside the kitchen window hummingbirds hover by the bright red feeder. Stuart watches them absently for a while. Then he stands and slowly rears his shoulders back. Fran goes into their room to find another shirt.

"Okay," he concedes as he fastens the pearly snaps. "Tell Kevin to go into town for that Co-op order. Get him to stop by the vet's on the way in, he can hear almighty Dickson's opinion and call home. And tell him not to waste any time." He tucks the shirt in and says flatly, "What the hell."

◆ ◆ ◆

Stuart goes out to the machine shed, starts the Massey-Ferguson, and backs it around to hitch up the swather.

He keeps the tractor in second gear because the crop is so thick he's afraid it could plug the rollers. The serrated teeth on the cutting head bite cleanly into the mature stems, clicking efficiently, and leave behind a neat and even stubble. The grill of the Massey pushes against the heads of grain. Barley kernels bounce hard off the faded engine cowling, off the high back fenders, and the whirling tines behind fling them up at Stuart's red neck. The first round of the big field seems decades long. He recalls the lather on the horses the first time he worked that ground, when it was nothing but a wild meadow, and they pried up the sod a stride at a time.

That was thirty-odd years ago. He and Fran reached the Cariboo in their road-weary Ford, with all that was left from Montana in the truck's small box. That first bad winter (was it '57 or '58?) was so cold it cut his lungs, and the snow drifted so high from the north side he couldn't see the cabin. Moose ate half his hay that year. Not near so many folks in the valley then, but closer ties, summer picnics, and horse races down on the river flat. Stuart ran a liver-coloured gelding once, a bat-brained colt, but he'd give Wilson and them fifty yards head start and then fly on past, laughing fit to bust and flapping his hat in the air.

Now, in June they help him with his branding, and cutting the calves, and then there's always a barbecue. Fran prepares for days beforehand. Stuart grills the steaks. Last month, during that barbecue, a rented Lincoln pulled into the yard. A German tourist got out and offered him a million dollars for the operation. Just like that. None too politely, Stuart declined.

The air is rich with the taste of green grain, and nitrogen. He completes two rounds, then raises the cutting head, disengaging it while he turns the tractor around to begin the backswath, the outermost cut. Now he goes slowly, carefully watches the outside wheel of the machine in the rougher ground. He doesn't see the rusted hitch bar hiding in the grain. The jutting teeth scoop it up and it jams in the rollers of the swather. The unit bucks and clangs and flies half to pieces before Stuart can shut it down.

A stealthy wind carries off the last mutter of the Massey's diesel engine and the exhaust cap falls shut. Stuart shoves his hat back, and for a moment just slouches in the seat.

He is slow to inspect the swather because he knows it's bad. He'll have to take it into Williams Lake to be rebuilt and find another in the meantime to finish the field. He swears, but weakly, out of habit—tries to feel more anger and less fear creeping up on him. What the hell, he can borrow Wilson's old rig, it isn't that serious. But he finds himself in a hurry to get back to the house. The air is muggy, and clouds are coming over the ridge.

◆ ◆ ◆

The kettle is whistling. Stuart steps in through the back door and picks up the phone in the hall.

"Can't you shut that damn noise off," he shouts at Fran. "I've got to make a phone call!" When the whistle continues he slams down the receiver and barges into the kitchen. "Listen I —"

His wife is stretched out on the linoleum, a blank stare in her hazy, fading green eyes.

Stuart has known death for fifty years. He has always accepted it, like he accepts the weather and the government. But he's down on his knees now and whispers, "Hey Fran? Fran, honey? Franny!" Coarse panic infuses his voice. The kettle screams until it is dry and then begins to smoke. Finally the stench of charred metal pierces his shock; wearily he stands to push it off the element. Then Stuart takes a woollen comforter from the couch and wraps his wife in it. Dumbly, with difficulty, he lifts her from the floor and carries her down the narrow stairs to the root cellar, where his shoulder bumps a side of bacon hanging on a hook. The meat sways and its shadow crosses the wall like a black wing. He lays Fran's body on a plank shelf next to her own jams and canned vegetables. The beans had been good the year before; so there are many jars of these, and peas, and the tiny dilled carrots that Stuart likes so much.

♦ ♦ ♦

Hailstones clatter on the roof. Vivid green branches of the weeping birch lash at the front room window. The Heeler bitch is howling in the yard. Stuart goes outside leaving the door open. He stands on the porch and watches the grain fall in dark sweeping crescents under the hail. It will rot.

He turns back into the house and walks through to their bedroom. From the top drawer of the colonial dresser he lifts an object wrapped in oily flannel cloth, and then a box of cartridges. The pistol is a nickel plated Smith & Wesson, with an ivory grip, which the grateful council of Miles City had awarded his grandfather, a seasoned lawman Stuart's father could never stand up to. Stuart loads five chambers, leaves the hammer on the empty one as Grandpa always said to do. Viciously he sweeps the tartan linen off the dresser, and all the old family photos skitter across the floor. He catches his own reflection in the antique mirror. His eyes are frenzied, his silver mustache is wet with tears, and he laughs out loud.

Sharp fragments of clear sky are left, as if the maelstrom dropped from space, smashing the fragile blue shelter that had protected the valley. In his long slicker, with one hand on the crown of his hat, Stuart fights his way into the heaving field. His boots snag in the twisted stems of the broken oats and barley. Hail glistens in drifts on the matted, darkening grain. Driven by a terrible elation he kicks his way forward to stand in the middle of those ninety acres. With his legs widespread, the bright yellow coat flapping behind him, he lifts up his eyes and shrieks into the glare of the lightning. He throws open his arms. His old Stetson is sucked out into the universe. And in one fluid motion he draws the gleaming pistol from his belt and turns it accusingly on the sky. Stuart fans the hammer five times, so rapidly just one vain bark of gunfire precedes Heaven's reply.

THIS IS HOW IT IS

Clover thistle clay primed '58 chevy aspens wire hose fence tricycle toolshed firewood spruce

He does not want to phone. But this is how it is: he's expecting his daughter Joni to be dropped off for the weekend, any minute, but it's been more than an hour now. He'd planned to put the casserole in just after Joni arrived, so she could see it, pretend she helped because she says it's her "best supper." Then they'd have half an hour in the yard to play, chat about their weeks apart, hear

whatever words she's learned, things she's done, maybe things
Mommy said.

*arborite cream phone black apples crayons rodeo calendar stainless
photos child granny linoleum sportbag hardhat dogdish*

The casserole is in the oven, the table set for two. Steve leans
against the jamb of the open patio door, alternately watches the
driveway, the telephone, studies his backyard, considers what
improvements he can manage this summer, or afford, and why his
ex-wife has not arrived or at least called, goddamn it. He does not
want to phone.

*mile strip grass reach reeds reserve 60 kmh churches jackpines tongue
leftright lakeside neon daylight vacancy childless junction chrome
sage*

Tuna Potato Chip Casserole

1 can flaked tuna
1 small bag potato chips
1 can cream of mushroom soup
Arrange layers of tuna, potato chips & soup in greased pan. Sprinkle
with crumbled potato chips. Bake at 350 ° for 30–35 min.

oven margarine finger skipjack brine enamel salt minutes chips pan bits palm water skin heat

Custody was decided last fall, in Angela's favour, with allowance for his rights, every second weekend and certain holidays. Steve has tried to accept it. What's been hardest is the idea of Jerry taking his place. He and Jerry were never friends, but knew one another from the bar. That's how Steve always saw Jerry: playing pool, drinking beer. So now he cannot, no matter how he works at it, accept the fact that Joni lives with Jerry.

After Angela first left, Steve was drunk most nights. Following his first visit with Joni —which involved hours of he and Angela yelling back and forth on the phone, and finally a social worker's help to arrange —he swore off alcohol. Prior to the separation he'd never been a heavy drinker. But now he quit it completely, for Joni.

On several occasions, Steve had asked Angela to reconsider or at least drop Jerry, for Joni's sake.

"Don't tell me about *my* life, or *my* daughter, Steve," she said over the phone. "You always had to have things your way. Who can live with that? So don't go blaming me for all this shit now."

One evening Joni mentioned that Jerry had slapped her. Steve immediately picked up her coat, her stuffed cat, and took her over to his mother's place.

"What's going on?" his mother asked, her attention fixed on her son's quiet ferocity. "Steve, please...."

But Steve was out the door, roaring across town, to the trailer where Angela and Jerry lived.

His ex-wife stood with her back against the closed door. He paced the small porch while they argued. Finally Jerry stepped outside.

"We can handle this!" Angela warned, putting her hand up against Jerry's chest.

"No," Steve yelled. "I'll ask him!"

"Ask what?" Jerry taunted, brushing Angela aside. "I'll ask you something, buddy—What the fuck is your problem?"

Steve swung at him. But he was no scrapper (Jerry outweighed him by forty pounds) and Steve took a beating. Neighbours watched it all.

The incident came up in court. According to Angela's testimony, it seemed clear that Steve had provoked the violence.

saws shriek remote operator yellow buckets forks halogen pepsi wrangler travel dust adult carpets steak pasta rattlesnakes bleach sky freezer canadian tire shrubbery radiator dualwide pigweed magazine helicopter tuna

Now he goes into Joni's room, pushes the curtains aside, opens a window, dusts the night table and dresser top with his sleeve. A pair of her little blue jeans, socks and three t-shirts are tossed on the bed. He did laundry Monday night. Now he folds the clean clothes, sniffs the softener, places them in dresser drawers.

He thinks he hears a car turning. No. Well, soon. He'd better set the table, slice a tomato. She loves tomatoes.

wedding dog highway gifts weekend meat milk creosote iwa carwash
sixfortynine prenatal fir bark dot roadblock macks western stars
asphalt pentecostals charcoal timothy latex

Receiver to his ear, Steve lifts what's left of the calendar year and, while repeated rings sound on the other end, lets months fall, stares at rodeo photos, broncs in mid-air, bulls and clowns, a blonde woman bent over the neck of a racing sorrel.

"Yeah, hullo."

He freezes hearing Jerry's voice.

"Hullo!" Jerry demands again, hurried, breathing hard.

"I'd like to speak with Angela."

"HA! Steve, buddy, 'course you would. But she's already out waitin' in the van. We're headed to the coast for the weekend."

"So you're dropping Joni off on your way?"

"No, no, kid's coming with us."

"What do you mean? Listen, can I please speak to Angela? She knows Joni is supposed to spend this weekend with me, I talked to her Tuesday—"

"Don't fuckin' know nothin' about that, buddy. Nice chattin' with you."

"Wait! This was arranged," Steve says, stressing his words. "I talked to Angela on Tuesday — "

"Tough shit."

Cut off, he stares at the white plastic receiver. He slams it against its cradle and drops his head on his arm, gasping. In seconds, rage has exhausted him. For a minute he leans there, shoulders heaving.

The kitchen reeks of baked tuna, but it does not occur to Steve that the casserole is past done.

He pushes up off the counter, grabs his keys. A few steps and he's out the patio door, behind the wheel, fumbling, swearing, twisting the key and gunning the engine.

But the moment before he slams the car into gear, his half-cocked plan unreels. He sees Joni's face, her confusion, tears, her light brown eyes fearful. He sits there, engine screaming, going nowhere.

In the oven, the casserole continues to cook.

shovel capsule mailbox semiautomatic bcr haze heron woman forklift banding broadway fireweed man muggy loony lily dental tumbleweed submarine drugmart leftright appliances lumber petrocan grass mile strip

At twenty past three Steve parks the forklift back of the mill maintenance shop. Oiled gravel dust sifts onto his lips, his boots swing out the cab door.

In the lunchroom he gulps water from the fountain. Then he stows his gloves, safety glasses, hard-hat and Thermos in the soiled sport bag he carries back and forth to work. Andy and Warren are already positioned near the door, watching the clock.

"Gristlehead get you to clean up the chain?" Warren asks.

"Yeah," says Steve, approaching the door.

"That's the press helper's job, and that prick knows —"

"Close enough," Andy interrupts, and pushes open the shop door.

The horn blows just as the three men reach the parking lot, divide, go separate ways to their vehicles. Forty-odd workers file out of the mill behind them.

Steve turns left onto the highway, right at the junction, joins the afternoon traffic's southern escape, pushing the speed limit. It's his weekend with Joni. He plans to make her favourite supper.

Once home he lets the dog out of the basement, drops his sportbag at the top of the stairs, pours himself a glass of iced tea and drinks it while resting his weight against the fridge. From one cupboard he takes a can of tuna, a can of mushroom soup. In another cupboard he looks for potato chips, preferably plain, but finds only sour cream and onion which hopefully won't matter. She'll be there in half an hour or so. He leaves the tuna, soup and chips close together on the counter, and goes to take his shower.

For many minutes he simply stands under the shower, letting the heated stream pelt his face and chest. Wondering about the time, he reaches for shampoo, hastily lathers his hair.

THIBEAU'S CROSSING

Yesterday they reached their verdict. Radio said the jury took hardly an hour to declare him not guilty. Rob Tanner is a free man, or as free as you can be with a thing like that on your conscience.

If you lived around here you'd know all about it. The Wendland-Tanner affair was big news over the past year. Only other thing I recall hearing much about was the mill chemicals in the river, but really we've known about that for a long time. There were people who weren't sure where Thibeau's Crossing was until we had our trouble.

Back in the old days, this was a shortcut to the goldfields. A Frenchman had set up below the bend and started rafting miners across the river. Later, the government put in a cable-ferry. Now, there's a stout one-lane bridge. No store or service station, just the various ranches in this valley, and the few of us that hold onto the mortgages and try and earn an honest living. Carl Wendland, who was my friend, used to say that none of us were rich, but we shared a wealth of peace hereabouts. And I believed him then.

The wife made a good brisket stew last night, with dumplings. When supper was done our two boys went off to watch the television, and we talked over the trouble while she washed the dishes. She says it's just as well Rob Tanner got off, that there was nothing to be gained by him going to jail. He'll suffer enough in his own mind, that verdict was the Lord's will, or so she figures. But she knows Lou-Ann pretty well, that's the woman Tanner had been living with, so it stands to reason she'd think that way. I didn't bother bringing that up, just let her have her say. But I've been thinking about it some more today, the whole mess.

◆ ◆ ◆

Wendland's ranch is right across the river from ours. It's for sale now. Last fall Bev sold all the stock and she and her kids moved away, over to Calgary, someone said. She was back in town this last week for the trial, but we didn't visit. I don't believe she even drove out here to look over her property.

No one seems certain whether Tanner is still living with Lou-Ann Black. I haven't seen his pickup by lately. Lou-Ann's place is across the river also, seven miles up the valley road from the Wendland spread. Carl Wendland was business partners with

Rob Tanner. They bought a D8 Cat and some other equipment between them. Carl was ranching full-time, but he invested in the machinery to clear his own land. When they were done with that, Tanner started his contracting jobs.

I'd say I knew Carl real well, and I know Rob Tanner well enough. And right now I admit that if I'd been either one, in their place, I might have done the things they did. But most of us steer clear of such situations. Like the wife says some people have certain leanings. I would guess Tanner did. Maybe Bev did too.

◆ ◆ ◆

It's surprising Wendland's ranch hasn't sold. Mainly the place is good level ground. There are irrigation lines for two of the fields, and they do a sight better than on this side of the river. Of course the real estate people are still asking a good dollar, three-quarter million, I believe. Not many individuals with that kind of money want to work in boots fifteen hours a day.

Actually, I believe Carl had some money from somewhere to begin with, so you might say he had a head start on ranching. But he worked hard too. And he was generous. Truth is he was real generous to us in particular, but he never made you feel obliged. Last June my old baler busted down, and I couldn't afford to even rent another one. When Carl found out he brought his own rig over the same day.

Folks around here respected Carl Wendland. He represented our valley at the Cattlemen's Association meetings, and he had friends in government. Mind you, one person meant as much to him as any other. At social get-togethers he was the guy who'd start things off. He loved a good joke. Not that he went around with a grin on all the time, but when he smiled it was wide and well-meant. Funny thing, he was the only guy I've ever known that favoured yellow shirts. And he was big. Not so big as I am, or quite as heavy anyway, but plenty strong. So when he took after Rob Tanner it was bound to be ugly.

Lou-Ann testified that Tanner was in pretty rough shape before he grabbed the shotgun. It was an antique, silver inlaid thing that he used to like to show off. Maybe Carl would have killed him, I can't say.

Apparently Lou-Ann was running for the phone when she heard the shots, or one shot. The Crown Counsel called that a discrepancy. He said there was some differences between what Lou-Ann told the RCMP at first, when they got to her place, and then what she said in court. The question still being, whether Tanner triggered both barrels together, or one at a time. "What does it matter in the end?" the wife says.

It gets me downright mad how people talk. Since the fight, Tanner's face hasn't been quite the same, but still they always have to call him "a handsome man." Now I don't see why that particular fact matters at all. Same way as I don't see the point in all the chrome on Tanner's pickup, or the expensive Stetsons he likes to wear, but that's the kind of character he is. To be honest I can't say I understood why he and Carl were friends. I never felt easy when I was with the two of them together, but Carl and I got along just fine. Tanner is different. There are a few fine Quarter-horses up at Lou-Ann's and he used to spend his weekends cutting or calf-roping. He was even a bull-rider for a time, and he still likes to look the part with his fancy boots and handle-bar moustache.

The other day Dianne Wilson was over for coffee, which happens a bit too often for my liking. She and the wife were in the kitchen, and I don't think they heard me come in. I was still in the porch, just about to take off my rubbers, when I heard Dianne's smart voice saying how she couldn't blame Bev— something about "plain old Carl all the time," and Rob Tanner and "bedroom rodeo." I stepped back outside then and closed the door real quiet. It was a cold day for March, but clear and sunny, with light glaring off the ice in the yard. I went back to what I'd been doing, cleaning out the feedsheds, hearing the wife laughing after Dianne's joke.

◆ ◆ ◆

Sometime ago we converted the old ferry house by the bridge into a kind of community hall. Carl and I did a lot of the work, and Wilson, and Lyle Keller. Tanner helped some, though he isn't much of a carpenter—we all have our talents. We just knocked out a couple of walls, put in new windows, and a bit of a bar. Generally we'd have get-togethers spring and fall. There'd be a barbecue going, maybe a pot of chili, and salads and pies. Everybody brought a cooler of beer, and we'd play horseshoes or softball until it got dark. Then we'd turn the lights on, and there'd be music, and dancing after a while. You might not guess it looking at me, but I like to dance. It's good to remember all of us dancing, couples bumping into each other, laughing, and singing together. And Carl stompin' around the floor in his yellow cowboy shirt.

It was that night last spring, though, when I got my first hunch there might be trouble. Now that I think on it, maybe I should have done something.

I don't drink much, but I'd had a few beer and it was time for a walk out back. It's fairly open between the cottonwoods along the river so I went down to the edge of the bank. The moonlight crossed the slow current in the water, and it was real pleasant just standing there.

Heading back to the hall I heard a woman laugh, playful like, over in the shadows. Well I knew right off it was Bev. I was in good spirits, and I piped up and said, "Now what are you two up to out there, eh?" There was no answer, so I just chuckled to myself and went on in. The room was hot and noisy, somebody had cranked the music up, and I even recall the song. It was Waylon Jennings singing "Good Hearted Woman," and my wife and Carl Wendland were dancing.

It was a while later that I noticed Tanner step inside. He went by the bar, then walked over and handed me a beer. He grinned and said, "Slim, you're looking thirsty." I only remember that because as a rule he had nothing to say to me. And I don't mind most folks calling me Slim, but I didn't like it coming from him.

♦ ♦ ♦

Last August was hot and dry, but mostly overcast. We kept looking for rain but it didn't come. I was irrigating the bottom field, trying to get some kind of second crop. One evening while

I was out moving the pipes Wendland's pickup pulled in by the gate. Carl got out and walked over, looking mighty tired, but he pitched in and helped me change the line. When it was set we walked over to the head valve and I opened her up. That's always good, to hear the nozzles spit, and then see the first water hit the dry ground.

Carl hadn't said much. But he was generally too busy just to wander over for a visit, so I was waiting. While we stood watching the sprinklers kick in, one after the other, he told me. Two weeks earlier he had stopped by Rob Tanner's place, in the middle of an afternoon, and found Bev alone with him there. Since that day, Carl said, he'd felt a hundred different emotions, but mostly *hate*. He used that word like I'd never heard it used before. He was worn out, leaning against the fence, talking a bit at a time. I was quiet. When his face started to tremble I put my arm over his shoulders.

Across the river I could see the big light in Carl's barnyard. We were standing on my land, with the sprinklers whispering behind us. Only a half-mile from the house, and it seemed like the middle of nowhere.

All I could think of was to pray. So I started, out loud, while Carl cried with his head on his arm.

For weeks afterward, he struggled to keep that hate down. Carl had never gone to church while I'd known him, but I took him into town one night to talk with our minister. He told me that it helped. September came, and things weren't back to normal, but they seemed to be settled, like I said in court. Then on the night of the eighteenth Carl had a few drinks of scotch, got into his pickup, and went charging up to beat the stuffing out of Tanner. It was over before Lou-Ann called the RCMP. From across the river we heard their car go by, because they had the siren on. I don't know why. That was the first time I could remember hearing one in our valley.

Last night I just let the wife have her say. I sure don't claim to know all what is right and wrong, especially when it comes to law and discrepancies, or situations people get into. But I'm having a darn hard time believing that the verdict, or any of it, was the Lord's will.

CHARITY

The congregation knew her story soon enough. The all-time attendance record at the Fraser Baptist church was one hundred and eighty-three, set the previous Easter, but on your average Sunday morning it was half that number, even less during the summer months with folks taking holidays, horse shows every other weekend, and the local golf course in its best shape. The inner circle was small enough that any worthy rumour made the rounds within the space of seven days. So, after Shawna Psalzer came with her kids two Sundays in a row, word about her got around.

There was a goodly amount of sympathy. In the foyer after the service Carol Barnes, the pastor's wife, made a point of taking the younger woman's hand in welcome. And, following her lead, a number of other church women did the same.

Shawna Psalzer's husband had been involved in a terrible accident, a head-on collision which left two other people dead and himself in a coma. The newspaper noted that alcohol had been involved, Psalzer and his buddy having left the bar shortly beforehand, in his pickup. Apparently the lone driver of the other car was a tourist pushing through the night intent on reaching his destination, perhaps dreaming of it, or of the woman he was meant to meet there, moments before he was decapitated by the chrome bumper of a 4x4.

Shawna was left with three kids, a thirteen year old boy by a different father, and Tony's girls aged nine and seven. No sort of insurance. Fortunately she had a job, as a sales clerk in a clothing store.

Following the accident, almost fifteen years after she'd briefly attended a young people's group at the Fraser Baptist, she went back to the church. The other women welcomed her, bestowed their charity, some were even quite sincere about it.

♦ ♦ ♦

They had gone through numerous pastors at the Fraser Baptist over the last decade, none of them lasting more than a couple of years, for various reasons. One spoke too much fire and brimstone; the next was fresh out of theological college and had the gall to suggest Genesis be read as allegory; the next was not satisfied by the salary; finally there was the yokel from Saskatchewan who wore the same brown suit with a clip-on tie every Sunday.

Phil Barnes struck the balance. He wore steel grey or dark blue, and smiled in a manly way. (Some of the women said he smiled like Robert Duvall, as much with his eyes as with his mouth.) He appeared conservative, yet open-minded at the same time. First summer he was here he organized the congregational softball tournament, which became an annual event. He was a pretty fair ball player too. His sermons drew from both testaments, and sometimes from events in the world news. His wife, Carol, was a gracious, attractive woman, who involved herself in church activities without stepping on any toes. They had four children, three teenage boys and a younger girl who sang like an angel.

♦ ♦ ♦

"Good morning Mrs. Psalzer," the pastor said through the screen door.

It was a blustery day in April, with dirty pyramids of snow still melting slowly in the shadows at the side of the house. Her place was older, showing some neglect, with a half-stripped pickup sitting in the carport, the front axle on a stack of planks. It was one of several houses along a sloping crescent street, which years ago might have been quite a pleasant neighborhood in view of the river, but was now abutted by an industrial strip. In fact it was at the very edge of a mill yard where spruce logs were heaped in ridges. The pastor took this much in as he parked his maroon Buick in the driveway. He reached for his leather case, chose at the last moment to leave it in the car. With just his Bible in hand he walked up the scuffed wooden porch steps, hesitated half a moment, knocked.

She'd been expecting him. He called yesterday to extend the offer of a visit.

"Hi," she says, her hand at the screen latch. "Come on in," standing aside to let the pastor through the doorway. He pauses to remove his shoes.

"Oh don't fuss about that, please." She gestures at a chair by the table. A blue cloth has just been laid, the neat fold lines plainly visible. There is a plate with some baking set out. "Would you like coffee?"

"Thanks, that would hit the spot," he replies although he needs no more. This is his second visit of the day and he drank two cups at the last house. She places another steaming mug in front of him. He helps himself to a spoonful of sugar.

The pastor spends three days a week visiting members of the congregation. His wife suggested he visit Shawna Psalzer, to speak with her of the Holy Spirit. The kitchen is clean, though the pattern is worn off the linoleum and the walls are yellowed. There's a scent of cigarette smoke, although no ashtray on the table. A cat's food and water dishes are set on a newspaper beside the moaning fridge.

This is part of his job. He has shared in the grief of many families over the years. It calls for a sensitive approach, usually the willingness and patience to listen. People sometimes grow angry: *Why has this happened?*

Shawna Psalzer seems comfortable enough, or at least not displeased to have him there. She doesn't say much. She's a rather small-framed woman, wearing a faded sweatshirt and blue jeans, moccasins for house slippers, bit tired maybe. She has thick black, finely curved eyebrows.

As if just friends they chat about their children and the unpredictable spring weather. Only last week there was a late snow, now the first green blades are peeking up through the unraked lawn. The pastor poses a few careful questions, but she avoids any reference to her husband's accident. She doesn't seem distraught, or fragile. An overcast, mid-morning light is suspended in the kitchen windows. She seems, in a curious way, too calm.

The pastor reaches for the offered baking, eats a slice of lemon bread, one cookie, then another. He's used to gently guiding a conversation, but she unnerves him slightly. Fig newtons. Little squares, dark and rich. He should say what he came to say, he tells himself, mouth firmly closed, nibbling tiny seeds between his front teeth. He touches the black Bible gently with his left hand, takes a sip of coffee and is prepared to broach the matter. He's opened his mouth to speak when Shawna, who has not been looking at him, stops him with a question.

"Do you ever think how life would be different if just one thing hadn't happened?" she glances into his eyes and away, runs a finger back and forth along the table's edge.

The pastor shuts his mouth and watches her for a moment. He's unused to questions about himself on such occasions.

"We all do, I believe, from time to time. And it isn't always easy to sort these things out on our own."

"Oh I don't expect to sort much of it out," she laughs, her teeth protruding slightly, "but some days I have to wonder."

"Yes...," he nods. He does not make his usual reference to the role of the Personal Savior, etcetera, cannot bring himself to say what he should. "These are very tasty," he says instead, reaching for another Fig Newton, "and I haven't had one for ages."

"Yeah, the kids don't fancy them, so it's something I can usually find in the cupboard. Always loved them myself." The pastor gets a glimpse into her mouth, her teeth and tongue poised, just before she bites.

Their discussion wanders. She has a habit of looking off to the left as she speaks, not facing him. This heightens his own attention, and each time their eyes do meet he receives a tiny shock.

"Oh," he starts, reading the clock on the stove, "I hadn't noticed the time. I'm afraid I have another appointment at eleven."

It's quarter to the hour. Fired by caffeine and an odd nervousness the pastor leaps to his feet, grabs his Bible. On the porch, feeling slightly rude or unsatisfied by his counselling, he turns and says, "So, Wednesday is your regular day off. Would you like me to drop by again next week?"

"Ah, sure. That'd be nice," she smiles, holding the screen door open for a moment against the spring breeze.

◆ ◆ ◆

Shawna imagines Tony lying there. Where does the imagination go when it's confined in a coma? Does it foray out through the life-support lines, or curl up like a surly badger to hibernate?

Along the highway outside the hospital local traffic starts with logging trucks snorting out to the bush at two a.m., shiftworkers headed for the mills by six, then business and government people, then bankers and hairdressers. The river rolls south, surges over its crust of ice, sweeping stray logs, miscellaneous objects, a few green trees felled by its forceful undercut against the banks. Geese angle north. Blind animals are born underground.

◆ ◆ ◆

There had been no change in Tony's condition. Nothing was certain, but the neurologist had confided that any chances of recovery were slim. The pastor learned this from Shawna on his second visit.

She was clearly less tired, wore a flowered blouse which accentuated her breasts, faded jeans again. There were fig newtons set out on a blue rimmed plate. Again, despite a moment of prayer in the privacy of his car earlier on, the conversation veered its own way, a bit beyond the pastor's control. They talked about common things, how her kids got along in school, his own. As it turned out her son played hockey at the same level as his two youngest boys.

"Ah ha, I thought I recognized you," he said. "I mean that first Sunday you came to the church, your face seemed familiar. Maybe we were at some of the same games last winter?"

"Could be," she nodded, while gazing out the window. "I went sometimes to watch Alan play. Partly cause Tony never bothered. He and Alan didn't get on very well. Do you mind if I smoke?" The way she threw the question in took him off-guard.

"Ah, no, of course not."

"I've been trying to quit," she said, rising to fish a silver package of cigarettes, her lighter and an ashtray from a drawer, "but haven't quite done it."

They chatted for almost two hours, long enough for the pastor to eat half a dozen Fig Newtons. Shawna smoked four cigarettes. He was attentive to the practised gestures involved, as he wasn't used to smokers. As she inhaled, he noticed a slight dark down over her upper lip. And he became a bit self-conscious while chewing the soft cookies.

Her children arrived home from school, the two young girls giggling over something. When they saw him they hushed and were shy for a moment or two, then ran into the next room and resumed laughing. By contrast the boy seemed sullen. He was fair, or pale, and much slighter than the pastor's own sons. Alan was thirteen, and his chin and forehead were dotted with pimples. Unlike his mother, his moody eyes immediately locked with the pastor's own.

Phil soon excused himself, realizing with an inner puzzlement that once again he had delivered very little in the way of spiritual help. From the bottom of the porch steps he turned to say, "Please feel free to call, if you'd like me to stop by again."

"Thank you," she smiled, "I'll do that."

And she did.

♦ ♦ ♦

As a theology student, Phil had had an afternoon class with Dr. Rudolph Kraig, a course on the Gospels. Dr. Kraig was a distinguished elderly professor, but becoming senile. He regularly lost track of his lessons, sometimes filling out the hour with stories of the years he spent as a missionary. For a time he'd been on an island near Borneo, one of the first whites to make contact with a tribe of cannibals living in the jungle. One of his colleagues had in fact been "stewed" by the cannibals, according to Dr. Kraig. These sort of digressions had won Phil's admiration.

After reading Matthew chapter twenty-one, verses twelve through sixteen, Dr. Kraig laid his Bible flat on the lectern, thought silently for two or three minutes, then began his analysis which somehow, as always, involved a host of tangential references, from political history to quotes from Albert Schweitzer.

But Phil, on this particular afternoon, was not following to the lecture.

Through the window of the classroom the sunlight played across the page of his own Bible, and he read on in Matthew, and discovered in the next verses the account of Christ cursing a fig tree. From that day on the withered tree was a crude drawing on the far wall of his mind.

◆ ◆ ◆

Shawna Psalzer and her children sat toward the rear of the chapel, respecting the frontal pews favoured by the tithe payers. During the hymn singing, a few people cast a glance their way, offering a compassionate smile.

They offered bags of second hand clothes for her children, which she accepted. They invited her to the weekly women's prayer meeting, and although she had not yet attended, someone always invited her again. The church women were not all of one mind regarding Shawna Psalzer. She didn't seem all that contrite, some noted. Some were jealous of her looks, the awareness she stirred in their men. Some were attracted to her themselves, looked upon her as they would an actress in a melodrama. For these reasons they were all interested to see her more safely within their fold.

♦ ♦ ♦

The pastor was reading the newspaper, his habit in the late afternoon. Each morning he picked up the paper from his front porch, folded it neatly, and laid it on the sideboard in the dining room. His day began with ten minutes of prayer, and twenty minutes of Bible study during which he had his first cup of coffee. A high-fibre breakfast, then onto God's work. Long ago he'd made the decision not to distract himself with worldly news in the morning.

Now he was reading his paper, sipping a blackberry sparkling water.

The aroma of fried porkchops drifted from the kitchen, where Carol was preparing their dinner.

"Phil?" she called out. "Are you there?"

"What is it dear?" he said, while continuing to read the paper.

"I thought I'd invite Shawna Psalzer and her children over for dinner one night this week. If that's okay with you?"

He lowered the paper. It was Wednesday. He'd been with Shawna not more than two hours ago. He forgot to answer his wife.

"Phil?" Carol queried, stepping into the dining room, looking to where he sat in his colonial chair pushed back from the head of the table. "I haven't called her yet, if you'd rather not. It might be nice though."

"Yes," the pastor finally said. "Of course. It's very kind of you to think of her. And it would be nice."

◆ ◆ ◆

Branches in bud swirled in mild winds. After school Alan raked the lawn for an hour each day, and the portion he'd done thickened with new green grass. Against the wooden handle his young hands blistered.

For weeks clouds raced across the sky, released the last of the cold rains. After the clouds passed and the sun struck the ground, steam issued up. The potent sunlight covered the lawns and fields and the golf course, sunlight shot through the runoff rippling in the ditches and gradually dried the town's unpaved ground.

◆ ◆ ◆

From the beginning, her voice seemed to wrap around him. Its frank tone and the double-edge of humour often bitter. Her laugh anchored him to the earth, to every sensation. One minute it was out of the question, a guilty thought, and the next her touch prompted an embrace.

During their third visit the pastor finally managed a degree of grief counselling. Shawna nodded quietly for a time. She toyed with a spoon and fingered the edge of the tablecloth, smoked her cigarettes. When their cups were empty she rose to get more coffee.

She did not sit down again, but stood near the sink, staring out the window as she spoke: "What bothers me most, it seems, is that I don't feel more. Or what I feel doesn't seem like real pain. Not like when my mother died. I cried for weeks then." She placed her hands against the stainless steel sink. "Sometimes this feels like relief as much as anything. Tony wasn't —"

She hesitated. The fridge continued its droning. Outside the branches of the tree in the yard swayed in the wind. He wanted to rise from the table, but held back.

"Tony had a temper. I don't mean he's a bad man, or that he deserved what happened. But it wasn't always easy, living with him, especially for Alan."

The pastor stood up from the table and stepped toward her. Stopped short. She turned, and saw his worry, smiled gently and touched his arm.

♦ ♦ ♦

Their embrace changes everything. This house, her house, the place she lives is suddenly vivid with detail. The mustard coloured fridge, its laboured rhythm, its still white interior where her milk and eggs and the usual staples occupy the wire racks, tiny triangles of brown catfood scattered on newspaper, milk across a photo of the mayor's smiling face. Nothing is ordinary: not the changing light in the window over the sink, the two small plants, the cactus and the shamrock on the sill, not the blackbirds perched in the dusted silver maple beyond the glass.

For hours at a time it's as if he simply sheds the self he's been living in for forty-six years. Her past, her experience varies so far from his own. The way she speaks is so unexpectant. She laughs often, sometimes with an edge to her voice, sometimes as a defense. She possesses hard wisdom, and while it saddens the pastor to see this, he's drawn in.

Her arms go up, her fingers lace around his neck as they kiss. The first time his own arms flutter clumsily in the air before coming to settle on her back, then her waist. The dark down above her lip is moistened by their mixing breath. Against his biceps he feels the stubble of her underarms, pulls her tighter to him. Nothing is said for the longest time, while she, finally, stares into his eyes. On later visits he picks her right up off the floor, her legs wrap round him, her laughter coils about his ears.

"I can't understand this," he gasps, gripping her thighs, his face perplexed in a frown.

"You understand everything else, of course," she grins at him, musses his hair, as he carries her through to the bedroom.

Her breath is smoky, her body lithe. The first time she takes his penis in her mouth, he rears back surprised, knocks his skull against the headboard. (This left a sore bump, of which he was all too conscious while delivering his sermon the following Sunday.) She covers his chest with kisses, bites his shoulder. His skin is stark white against her darker skin and from her breasts deeper coloured blossoms swell. Shawna shows him what pleases her, guiding him with her hands, so that, virtually for the first time, Phil knows himself as a lover.

Afterward they talk the situation over again, and again, and all but swear not to let it happen anymore. The mood of their parting is unsettled, but despite anxiety there's always a last tender smile. Until the next phone call, and the next Wednesday.

◆ ◆ ◆

18 Now in the morning as He returned to the city, He hungered.

19 And when He saw a fig tree in the way, He came to it, and found nothing thereon, but leaves only, and said unto it, Let no fruit grow on thee henceforward for ever. And presently the fig tree withered away.

—Matthew, chapter 21

Sitting behind the wheel of his parked car, Phil Barnes read these verses over again although he knew them by memory all too well, knew them from three translations. At Bible college the students were given grave cautions against reading out of context. The miracle described in Matthew 21:18-22 was sometimes cited to exemplify the power of faith. But why did Christ have to curse the tree, especially if figs weren't in season?

It was a Tuesday morning. The pastor was driving toward the old folks' home for his monthly visit there when he heard Shawna's panting cries as clearly as if she'd been lying in the backseat. He was aroused momentarily —then an icy sweat frosted his forehead. His maroon sedan cruised through a red light. Horns blared. He sped across the bridge, past the Sunset Lodge, no idea where he was going or what year it was or how on earth he'd gotten himself into such a predicament. Five miles up the highway, his arms shaking on the wheel, he turned at the entrance to Butte Park and drove up to the parking lot at the viewpoint.

"Dear Father," he prayed, aloud. He prayed hard for about ten minutes. There was no one else around.

Beneath the butte the landscape fell away. He looked far out over forested hills and patches of rangeland, followed the distinct line of aspen growth up the valley to where the great brown river, the region's main artery, curved into sight. This viewpoint was highlighted on any tourist map. It was a place the locals brought their visiting relatives. But teenagers had taken to holding weekend parties up there, and some said they had ruined the place. Last fall a girl had been raped inside a van while other youngsters were drinking beer not forty yards away. Rude graffiti was sprayed along a low stone wall at the butte's edge.

After a second session of prayer, Phil lifted his forehead from the steering wheel, took a deep breath, and pinched the bridge of his nose with two fingers. He pushed open the car door.

He walked along the escarpment taking in the view. The hills were dark, thick with protected spruce, fringed at lower elevation by aspen and birch in new leaf.

Why did Christ, the all loving, omniscient Savior, curse the tree?

Turning back toward his car, Phil noticed the charred remains of a weekend party fire, beer cans squashed in the gravel, a stark white wad of tissue. Something else. He bent closer. The thing lay there like a sloughed translucent skin.

"Oh Jesus," he whispered to himself.

♦ ♦ ♦

Her climax takes him with her in a rush, her voice and fingers, his body bucks with a furious pleasure. She falls forward on top of him, murmuring as her gasps subside, humming. Phil presses his lips to the soft indentation of her temple, her hair. Just before drifting off, he's conscious of their moment, much as though it's something stolen from the rest of the frantic world, hidden away between them, a shared breath.

♦ ♦ ♦

Alan made his way home along the street, his sportbag slung over one shoulder, having skipped his afternoon classes. He didn't feel well, he couldn't stand being at school anymore that day. He wasn't part of the crowd of kids who hung out downtown, couldn't think of anywhere else to go, so he wandered home. The early afternoon was bright under a May blue sky. Everything held more interest for him, the traffic and ordinary town activity, because he wasn't used to being out and around at that time on a weekday. He wasn't sure what he'd tell his mom, except the truth. He didn't feel well. The rake was propped against the fence of the front yard, marking the last strip of ground to be done. He'd be happy enough to do it now, but then his mom was sure to ask how come he was healthy enough to rake the yard but he was home sick from school.

The driveway ran alongside their neighbours' hedge. Only when he turned in off the street did Alan see the car that was parked there. Peering in the passenger window he saw a tan leather case and a black Bible flat on the seat.

He eased the screen door shut, and stood still for a full minute in the kitchen. The house was quiet, yet he sensed something like an echo of activity. He set his sportbag on a chair, cautiously walked down the hall.

The door to his mom's bedroom was half open. He saw her hunched over the man, her skin, saw the long arc and indent of her spine and the splay of her naked hips. The pastor's one arm lay across her back, the other was outstretched. Her head lay upon his chest, and as Alan watched, he gently kissed her hair. Then the man's eyes lifted and met his own.

♦ ♦ ♦

The Fraser Baptist congregation was proud of the new church building which had been completed two years earlier. Not too proud mind you, not boastful, they had not wanted an ostentatious structure: just a bigger, better insulated, carpeted, more functional church, located on more pleasant property than the stucco one which they had outgrown. That's what they got. Several of the men were in the construction business, so they supplied equipment and materials at cost. The new exterior was sided with oil-finished cedar. They managed to bring the whole job in at just under a half a million dollars. On the feature wall behind the podium was a large, contemporary stained glass window, featuring a cross amid spreading shafts of golden light.

At five to eleven the pastor sits alone in the small room off the podium wing, as he has done on a thousand Sunday mornings.

In stray moments he thinks of Dr. Kraig. He thinks of that condom in the blackened gravel, the taste of fig newtons, Shawna's scent. He thinks of the summer farm labour he had between his years at college, washing green hay dust from the hair of his arms at lunchtime, the tart lemonade, Shawna's scent. He bows his head, makes himself focus on the job at hand. A sermon from Second Samuel, an everlasting covenant, ordered in all things, and secured; two dozen per package in cellophane; for all my salvation and all my desire, will He indeed not make it grow? The organist concludes the piece she's playing within a minute before the hour. The pastor stands, and opens the door.

The deacons rise, followed by the rest, to sing: "Praise God from whom all blessings flow, praise Him all ye here below, praise Father, Son and Holy Ghost, Aaaaaaameennnnn."

The services obey a time-honoured pattern: the pastor's greeting and standing prayer, followed by a hymn, the week's announcements, often a special musical performance by a family, or trio of inspired faces, another hymn for all, occasionally two, sometimes a prayer, then a twenty-five minute sermon, a hymn, and always the brief, uplifting prayer to close. The predominant mood is one of stability. No outbursts of hallelujah or hand-clapping here.

The walls of the main chapel feature a row of tall, narrow windows and as the sun rises this morning they glow like fluted pillars of white stone.

When the third hymn concludes, while people are sitting down and getting set for the sermon, the pastor grips both edges of the lectern and leans over, evidently reading the underscored verses in his open Bible. In fact, at this moment he experiences a curious sensation of standing outside his own body, perhaps at the rear of the room, observing his physical self as he might observe a stage performer. He touches his forehead, the frontal curve of the skull, clears his throat.

Lifting his head, he sees that someone remains standing near the end of a middle pew. Shawna tugs at the boy's sleeve, but Alan shakes her off, pulls free and takes half a step into the aisle. People take notice. Some crane their necks to see what's going on.

The boy stares, rocking back and forth as if in the next moment he might leap either backwards or forwards, either escape outside through the mahogany doors or charge the podium and hurl himself against the pastor. Judging by the fury in his eyes, anything is possible.

There are murmurs, whispers, people looking from the boy to the pastor. What on earth?

The pastor is centred within himself now, in the muscle in his chest, in the depth of doubt, and his will is flagging before the rapt eyes of the congregation. For an instant he recalls the missionary stewed alive by cannibals and he wonders what happened to that man's faith in the final minutes. Was faith even an issue, was his own theology eclipsed by one silly, niggling question, or the memories intimate to skin?

MEN'S WEAR

after a fashion

The incumbent hunched over the bar, weight on his forearms, red striped tie drooping in a puddle of beer. Given this posture, the vacant stare, the grip on an empty glass, Andy the bartender would have refused to serve any other customer. But he'd known Marvin Lang for a decade, and knew he wasn't drunk, not yet anyway. The last of the election results were in, was all, and former councillor Lang was out.

Long-time supporters had crowded the Goldpan Lounge earlier in the evening, pressing close to Marvin Lang, shaking hands. Flag-sized posters of his likeness were tacked to the walls. Platters of chicken wings and coldcuts and nacho chips had been laid out. Marv had gratefully declined all drinks proffered, for fear of botching his victory speech. Just a few hours earlier.

Now it was down to an ordinary Thursday night's business in the Bedpan, as regulars had dubbed the place, plus a few diehard Lang voters mostly too loaded to remember why they had come. The campaign manager overdosed on Caesars and spicy wings and barfed all over the floor of the men's washroom.

"Sixteen years," Marv muttered finally, with a cruel half-smile, at this point sitting alone at the bar.

"What's that?" The bartender stepped over, thinking maybe he had missed an order.

"Sixteen years on council, Andy. And what does my experience count for? Sweet diddly tonight!" Marv upended his glass on the bar. He tightened his mouth and continued in a sing-song, "Re-cycling, re-zoning, re-vamping.... They'll re-think their new ideas in six months when the bills are due, when our goddamn taxes double."

"You shouldn't take it so personal, Marv," Andy offered gently, whisking the empty glass over to the dish track, wiping down the bar in front of Lang's elbows. "Hey, you've done your bit, nobody can argue with that. You must hold the record for time on council, that's nothing to sneeze at. How about one more drink, on the house?"

"No thanks," he sighed. With effort he rose from his stool, then adjusted his shirt cuffs. Across town, he knew, various victory parties were in full swing. His sole consolation was that his wife had died ten months earlier; at least Dorothy had not witnessed his defeat, she was spared this humiliation. There was no one waiting for him, not at home, not anywhere.

It had never been in Marvin's character to change his mind. But abruptly he slapped the bar. "On second thoughts Andy, I'll have that drink, a double rye and Coke thanks. What the hell."

◆ ◆ ◆

Lang's Men's Wear was one of our town's oldest businesses, located at the corner of Main Street and 2nd Avenue, opened by Marvin's father in 1951. Few living locals could recall a time when the store hadn't been there. For about thirty years it was one of only four places to buy men's clothes around here, the others being *Wally's Western Duds* and a couple of department stores which regularly changed names. During that time Lang's was considered the upper crust, meaning that it stocked suits and dress shirts and ties, as well as quality work wear, socks, the usual.

Building upon his father's reputation, Marvin Lang enjoyed the status of being one of Williams Lake's half-dozen most successful merchants for many, many years. In his mid-forties, looking for new challenges, he ran for one of five alderman seats, and won a place on the town council.

The men's wear business, as he soon grasped, fit quite naturally with politics. Men may not buy as many clothes as women, but they are every bit as vain. Between well-timed compliments and seasonal discounts, Marvin found it rather easy to win favour with the ranchers, the lawyers and realtors. By the next election his position on council was solidified, and every four years thereafter his seniority was pretty much taken for granted.

Lang's store was dry and quiet, and smelled faintly of wool. Rarely was there more than one customer at a time. Marvin had never chased after fashion, and was proud of that fact; his stock remained much the same year after year. Originally this made good business sense, because any sort of change is mighty slow around here.

But by 1985 or so, let's face it, even his faithful clientele began to consider Lang's a bit old fashioned. By then a few newer stores had opened, including *Work Wear House* in the mall. Marvin's sales declined. Luckily he paid no rent for the business, because he owned the building. His house was also long paid for, and as an alderman—or "councillor," as of 1988—he received a stipend of about ten thousand dollars. Financially he wasn't hurting, and perhaps only Dorothy ever knew how deeply the changing consumer trends affected his pride.

Realtors started dropping hints that the building, sitting smack in the commercial centre of town, would fetch a good price, hints about how he and Dot could retire down south, some little tourist village on the coast. Other would-be entrepreneurs approached him about leasing the space for a ski shop, a Native crafts gallery, a health food store.

"A health food store, for crissakes," he snorted to Dorothy, sitting watch by her hospital bed. "Says maybe a soup and sandwich bar too, vegetarian mind you. Where does he think he is? Damned if I'll sell out to some long-haired fairy like that!" He referred to the most persistent suitor, a fellow named Jeremy Wainscott, who wore his red hair in a pony tail and spoke in a voice too soft for Marvin's liking.

"Now, now, don't stew about it," Dorothy leaned forward in her hospital bed, patted his clenched hand. "It's a strain on your heart."

flakes were still falling when he arrived at the store that morning and began clearing the steps and sidewalk. The streets were quiet, with few braving the weather.

While he was busy with his shovel, one old fellow came shuffling along the sidewalk. Jimmy. He hung around the park or back entrance of the mall, a sullen drunk, known around town for causing trouble.

Marvin hesitated, Jimmy passed by without meeting his eyes. Marvin cleared his throat and said, "Good morning Jimmy."

The man stopped, turned slowly. Stiff unruly hair fringed his face. His shoulders were hunched, one arm across his front holding closed a threadbare jean jacket. He wore thin slacks, soiled down the thighs, and running shoes. His eyes were darkly glazed, but after a moment he nodded.

"Looks like we're in for another bout of winter," Marvin said, absurdly, as if Jimmy were an old buddy of his. Both men had been town fixtures for thirty years, but they had never spoken.

So Jimmy just stared at Marvin, waiting.

"Say, how 'bout some coffee? There's a pot just brewed inside, I'm on my way to have some. Damn cold out here. What do you think?"

"Coffee."

"That's right, come on," Marvin said, reaching for the glass door.

Jimmy took a slow glance up the street, the way he'd been headed. No appointments were pressing.

Marvin set out cups, stir-sticks and sugar cubes on his counter, and a quarter litre of cereal cream which he liked a dash of in coffee. Jimmy took his black with three sugars. They each drank a mug in silence. Outside the snow had nearly ceased. Jimmy's eyes slowly circled the room full of racks and racks of clothes. He nodded at the offer of more coffee, reached for sugar.

It was very quiet in the store. Marvin made two or three comments intended to spark some conversation, but each time Jimmy replied with a nod, or grunt, or nothing at all. Ten or fifteen minutes went by, with the coffee and stretched silence making Marvin a bit nervous. When Jimmy coughed Marvin jumped, and coffee sloshed on the counter. As he rose to wipe this up, Jimmy also got to his feet.

"Better get goin'," he said. "Good coffee. Thanks."

"You're welcome," Marvin said, cheered by these simple words.

As Jimmy made his way toward the door, Marvin noticed his denim jacket split across the shoulders. Near the front of the store stood a rack of coats, good coats, not one of which had sold that winter.

"Say Jimmy, wait a minute," Marvin said, catching up. "No offense, but your jacket sure has seen better days. What size do you take?"

Jimmy just stared at him.

"Your chest size? Thirty-eight, maybe forty?" Marvin selected a forest green size 40, pulled it off the hanger and held it out. "Try this one."

Jimmy shook his head, pulled his pants pockets inside out.

"Listen, don't worry about the money. Try it on." So Jimmy peeled off his jean jacket, and put his arms into the coat Marvin held open.

"How about that," Marvin grinned, guiding Jimmy toward a mirror. "Now this is light weight, but well insulated, made of highly water resistant material. And there's a hood rolled into the collar."

Jimmy studied himself in the mirror, then cracked a smile.

"Only problem is, it clashes something awful with those pants you got on. Let's see what else we can find." Marvin turned to the wide slanted shelves which displayed several brands of slacks, and chose some all-season khakis. From a rack of shirts he pulled a timeless plaid. A belt, t-shirt, some Stanfield underwear and a pair of wool socks completed the outfit, which piece by piece he'd piled in Jimmy's arms.

Jimmy stared at him, suddenly wary of some mean joke. "I got no money."

Marvin held his hands up, shook his head, not taking no for an answer. He pointed toward a cubicle. "You can change in there."

Five minutes later Jimmy emerged from the cubicle, moving cautiously in his new clothes. He stepped in front of the mirror, lifted his arms, turned and glanced over his shoulder for the rear view, then chuckled.

"Hey, hey, clothes make the man they say!" Marvin boomed. He tugged here and there, checking the fit, then fetched a pair of scissors and clipped the tags off the shirt and pants. "Too bad I don't have any boots," he said, "but wait a second —"

From a cardboard box he fished out a pair of galoshes. "There you go. Don't exactly match your shoes, but they're waterproof anyways."

"Okay man," Jimmy laughed aloud, fitting his runners into the rubber slippers. Their eyes met and held, "Could be you're goin' crazy eh?"

"Could be. Change is as good as a rest, they say."

"Anyhow... thanks."

"You're very welcome sir," Marvin smiled, holding open the door. "Tell your buddies to stop by, and we'll do what we can."

Jimmy nodded, laughing again as he left the store. He held his head higher and there was considerably more bounce in his step as he continued down the street.

Marvin rooted through the drawers of his old oak desk. Eventually he discovered what he was looking for, a crumpled piece of home-made stationary bearing Jeremy Wainscott's name and number. He might have thrown out the letter, except for the fact he rarely discarded anything. Dorothy had called him a pack-rat, and every few years would take it on herself to clean out the store desk. In the course of his search Marvin found several of Dorothy's own hand-written notes, only daily reminders and shopping lists and so on, but he set them carefully aside for safekeeping.

ACKNOWLEDGEMENTS

I've been fortunate to have had criticism and encouragement offered by several esteemed writers and editors, and to each of them I am deeply grateful. Thank you to long-standing friends, and to my family.

The Canada Council offered assistance by means of an Explorations Grant, which was much appreciated by the author.

◆ ◆ ◆

Stories in this collection were previously published, in some cases in different form or under different title, as follows.

"Heart Red Monaco" appeared in *Prism International* 30/4, Vancouver, 1992; selected for the anthology: *West By North-West: British Columbia Short Stories*, (D. Stouk & M. Wilkinson, Eds.) published by Polestar, 1998.

"The Next Nine Hundred Years" (as "Shifts") appeared in *The Fiddlehead* No. 178, Fredericton, 1994; selected for an anthology issue of Canadian stories for *Blue Moon Review*, WWW, (R. Cumyn, guest Ed.),1997.

"Horseshoes" appeared in *TickleAce No. 27*, St. John's, 1994.

"Come Evening" (as "Stream") appeared in *Pottersfield Portfolio* 16/1, Halifax, 1995.

"Scout Island" appeared in *The New Quarterly* XV/1, Waterloo, 1995.

"Taseko" appeared in *Event* 19/3, New Westminster, 1990.

"Let The Day Perish" appeared in *Event* 20/2, New Westminster, 1991.

"This Is How It Is" (as "Mile Strip") appeared in *The Fiddlehead*, No. 189, Fredericton, 1997.

"Thibeau's Crossing" appeared in *Whetstone* Winter issue, Lethbridge, 1996.

"Charity" (as "Fig Tree") appeared in *Prism International* 35/1, Vancouver, 1996.

Christian Petersen's stories have been anthologized in *Best Canadian Stories* 1997 (ed. by Douglas Glover) and *West By North-West: B.C. Short Stories*. He has published in *Event, Prism international, Pottersfield Portfolio, The New Quarterly, Grain, The Fiddlehead* and *TickleAce*. He has a BA in Writing from the University of Victoria and has worked with Jack Hodgins and Steven Heighton. He lives in Williams Lake, BC.